Elizabeth Gornac, a widow hard[ly]
[movi]ng into middle age, is at first so[lici]-
tous and later profoundly an[d]
[em]otionally moved by Robert, whose
[cu]rious charm stands in contrast to
[the] religious intensity of her own son,
[Pie]rre. Robert's presence, which has
[de]cisive effects on more than one life,
[is a] searing revelation to Elizabeth of
[th]e emptiness of her existence, in
[wh]ich even God is only numbness
[an]d sleep. The core of the book is
[th]e contrast, and the inevitable con-
[fli]ct, between those such as the Gor-
[na]cs who are born to work and those
[w]ho are born to love. In *Lines of Life*,
[th]e Nobel Prize winner has written a
[st]ory of dramatic and spiritual force.

LINES OF LIFE

FRANÇOIS MAURIAC

LINES OF LIFE

(Destins)

Translated by
GERARD HOPKINS

NEW YORK
FARRAR, STRAUS & CUDAHY, INC.

MANUFACTURED IN THE UNITED STATES OF AMERICA

LINES OF LIFE

LINES OF LIFE

I

"THE wind's cold. Haven't you got an overcoat, Bob? I'll
go and fetch mine."

The young man protested that he was stifling, but
could not stop Elisabeth Gornac from hurrying off to the house
with her rather lumbering gait. Over the hard earth, between
the hornbeams parched by the heat of the dog-days, she made
her painful way. It was as though her slim legs and small feet
were no longer strong enough to carry the weight of a body
which was verging on corpulence.

Bob grumbled to himself:

"I'm not all that ill. . . ."

All the same, sitting there on the sizzling flags of the terrace,
with nothing to support his back, his shoulders and his head, he
felt ill at ease. He was still weak enough not to like being left
alone. The spectacle of Elisabeth Gornac waiting at the far end
of the alley until the Catalan day-labourers, in their sulphate-
stained smocks, should have filed past her, made him impatient.
They stared at her but did not touch their hats.

'Really,' she was thinking; 'one doesn't know nowadays
whom one's got working on the place.'

But here, in the under-populated valley of the Garonne, the
vines must still be made to yield their fruit. Elisabeth was continually saying to her father-in-law, Jean Gornac:

"These precious Catalans of yours will cut our throats one of
these fine days. . . ."

All the same, she would have been as ready to take on a whole
gang of murderers if that had been the only way of keeping the

9

vines in health. Nothing must happen to *them*: they must always come first.

She caught sight of her father-in-law sitting, with his stick between his knees, in the courtyard round which the dilapidated château and its two wine-stores was built. His cheeks, and the sweat-soaked crown of his head were flushed, and the blood had caused the veins of his hands, of his exaggeratedly short neck, and of his temples, to swell.

"You *haven't* been down to the vines in this heat, surely, father!"

"You'd hardly credit it, my dear, but Galbert's actually been pruning, though I told him expressly not to! I suppose he thought I shouldn't go along and see what he was up to! . . ."

But she did not stop to listen. She went on into the house, leaving the old man to grumble at her. Never set eyes on her, these days, he didn't: she never stayed in one place long enough. Here she was now with a heavy coat over her arm: lucky she, to be feeling cold!

"It's not for me, it's for young Lagave. It'd be a terrible thing if he had a relapse. . . ."

She was already half running towards the line of hornbeams, and did not hear old Gornac's angry mutterings: – not a thought for anybody these days but that good-for-nothing young tailor's dummy!

'And to think that Maria Lagave, his grandmother, used to work for me as a daily woman, and do all the washing!'

But her son, Augustin, Bob's father, had made his way, by sheer hard work and determination, to a high position in the Ministry of Finance. Old Gornac forgot his anger: he could never help smiling when he thought of Augustin Lagave.

"Ah, Maria, where would your Augustin be to-day, if it hadn't been for me?"

Each time he put this question to his neighbour, she inevitably replied:

"But for your good advice, Monsieur Gornac, Augustin and I would be starving in some tiny parish of Sauterne or Les Landes."

No doubt about it, she had been an intelligent woman and fiercely ambitious for that son of hers who had been so good at his books. The curé of Viridis had got him a scholarship at the junior seminary. Peasant though she was, she had had every right, way back in the 'nineties, to think that a well-educated and well-behaved boy could do well in the Church. There was no lack of prosperous parishes where the priest's mother could grow old in comfort and respected by all.

But Jean Gornac, then in the prime of life, had seen which way the wind was blowing. Though he had never felt much love for the Church, it would never have occurred to him, at any other time, to play an active part against it. No doubt he had acquired a solid and traditional anti-clericalism from anthologies of Voltaire and the songs of Béranger: but, with his middle-class origins, he was not one to regulate his behaviour according to the dictates of any ideology. What he liked to think of as his religion of progress had looked like suffering a mild eclipse in May, 1877, but after the elections of the 14th October, he had given his support to the winning side, and had never afterwards left it. More than anything else, the collapse of the *Union Générale*, which had been no less a religious than a financial disaster, had contributed to strengthen his new loyalties. For years afterwards, Jean Gornac had felt himself go pale at the thought that if his devout, church-going father, who had died in 1881, had lived for a few months longer, the whole of the family fortune might have been swallowed up! He had had only just time enough in which to get rid of his Union

Générale shares, and his holdings in Banques Impériales et
Royales Priviligiées des Pays Autrichiennes, which had the
backing of the Union.

'And father might well have hung on for another year. . . .'

All the same, he never grew tired of saying to Maria
Lagave:

"It won't do any harm to let Augustin finish his seminary
training: it costs you nothing, and it will give him a footing in
the enemy camp."

He had sent his own two sons as boarders to the Diocesan
College at Bazas. The food there was better than in any of the
Secondary Schools; the boys got plenty of fresh air, and the
teaching was sounder.

He could still remember the blazing-hot day at the beginning
of August, when he had seen Maria Lagave get out of the train
at Langon, her best silk scarf tied round her head, and her arms
full of red-bound books and gilded green wreaths. Augustin
was following at her heels, tripping over the skirts of his first
soutane.

"I suppose we shall have to address you as M'sieur le Curé,
eh?"

"We shall have to treat you with proper respect, shan't we,
Augustin?"

Thus had the assembled boys and girls laughed at him.

Jean Gornac had very deliberately looked the other way. But
that same evening he had paid a call on the Lagave family,
where he was a familiar and authoritative figure. He sat himself
down without the slightest feeling of embarrassment at disturbing the family feast in honour of the boy who, in addition to
carrying off all the first prizes of his year, had won the Diploma
for Rhetoric. In vain did Maria Lagave protest that "they"
insisted on their philosophy pupils wearing the soutane, that it

would be time enough for him to leave it off when "they" should think about making him a tonsured priest.

"That shows how little you know about it, my good woman. Don't you realize that it will stick to him like glue? that the memory of all this will dog him always, and give him the reputation of being an unfrocked cleric?"

Before he would let them get on with their meal in peace, Maria had had to promise that the boy should resume his lay dress the very next morning. Jean Gornac had undertaken to provide him with a new suit, and to pay the fees for his philosophy year at the Lycée. But Maria had loudly bewailed the loss of the soutane – which "had cost a mint of money and been worn only for one day" – until he succeeded in convincing her, that it would make a lovely skirt for her:

"Feel the material: it'll last you a life-time."

Those years had been Jean Gornac's heyday. The bald, yellow-faced little man, with the bright and inexpressive eyes, had given only part of his time to the flourishing wine business which he ran in Bordeaux. In point of fact, he cared for money only insofar as it enabled him to buy more land. For some time now he had had his hands full with two distinct operations, the one financial, the other political. Parcel by parcel he absorbed the vast properties of the Sabran-Pontevès in Les Landes, and every four years he captured on hehalf of the Government, several hundred votes from the sitting member, the Marquis de Lur.

He was an object of admiration to his neighbours. He had founded a club at Viridis to which, each Saturday, after getting their pay, the field-labourers came to drink and talk politics. Cowmen and muleteers regularly dropped in there, and did not return to their farms until late in the night. The Good Fathers of Viridis got nowhere with their Guilds and their brass-band and their banners. Jean Gornac did not quarrel with them over the children. He knew that when the boys began to grow up, it would be easy for him to attract them to a place where they could drink as much as they liked, and talk about their exploits with the girls.

1893 was the year of Jean Gornac's triumph. The old vine-growers still talk about that blazing hot summer, and in the bottles which bear its date, the heat still glows. It reminds them how good life was in those days, when the delicious wine flowed in such quantity that it was left in the tun for lack of casks. A perpetual fire reddened the sky above Les Landes. That was the year in which the Marquis de Lur lost his seat, defeated by a lawyer from Bazas whose backer had been Jean Gornac. It was then, too, that the former seminarist, whom he regarded as his mascot and had helped with money from his own pocket, had competed for, and won, a place in the Inspectorate of Finances. To add to all this, Jean Gornac married his eldest son, Prudent, to Mademoiselle Elisabeth Lavignasse, only child of a family which, though less rich, was older and more highly thought of than his own. Finally, taking advantage of the fall in timber prices occasioned by forest fires, he bought for a song the last remaining acres belonging to the Sabran-Pontevès.

Now, at eighty, and rapidly approaching the time when he would go to his rest in the earth which he had loved so well, old Gornac dreamed of the great days when the harvests had been good, and there had been no lack of man-power to tend the vines. His grandson, Pierre, was for ever uttering jeremiads on the subject of depopulation. Had people really had more

children in 1893 than they did now? Whether or no, there had
been workers and to spare then! . . . He himself had given to
the world just precisely the two sons he had always meant to
have. It mattered little that his wife (a Péloueyre) had died after
the birth of the second: she had done what had been expected
of her. Two boys had been essential: one to look after the estate,
the other to make a living at the expense of the State. Still,
better to have one child than three or four. On that point Maria
and Monsieur Gornac were at one. What pleasanter sight than
several inheritances accumulating on a single head! One son
was enough, provided he lived on his land.

And so it was that when his daughter-in-law produced a
second son ten months after the birth of the first, Monsieur
Gornac was much aggrieved:

"My *louis* are worth no more than ten francs now" – he
grumbled.

When a third was born, he declared:

"My *louis* are worth only three francs now. . . ."

However, the two youngest died in childhood: one of capil-
lary bronchitis which the doctor treated with hot tea: the other
of dysentery, as a result of feeding on soup like its mother and
father.

It is doubtful whether old Gornac had admitted even to himself that his life had ceased, for several years now, to move
along the lines which he had laid down. His two sons had joined
the two young innocents in the cemetery, and all he had left
now was his daughter-in-law and a grandson, Pierre, who consistently got on his nerves. He talked about the boy as little as
possible.

Elisabeth Gornac hurried back to the terrace, where the handsome young convalescent, Augustin's son, Robert Lagave,

known to her as Bob, whom she had carried in her arms as a
child, was sitting. He had buttoned his jacket.

"You see, you *are* feeling the cold!"

She put her coat round his shoulders, and turned up the fur
collar. Far from showing the slightest annoyance, the young
man thanked her in a voice which seemed to show that he felt
touched by her attentions. Even when he was talking of the
most casual matters, his voice had the power to charm. There
was a slight break in it, as though its owner were not quite
grown up. His face, indeed, was not that of a man of twenty-
three. The fresh-complexioned cheeks looked hairless, and
there were patches of a rather too high colour on the cheek-
bones. He expressed his thanks with a rather self-conscious
smile, and she, after wrapping him up, moved a short distance
away from him. The long, thick, baby lashes imparted an almost embarrassing languor to his gaze. Elisabeth averted her
eyes, and fixed them on a train which was moving slowly
across the distance.

She had known Bob as a small boy, but this was the first
time, since he had turned fifteen, that he had spent so long a
time in the country. She had not yet had an opportunity to
notice that he looked in precisely the same lazy fashion at
people, dogs, stones and trees, or that this was entirely due to
those long, thick, straight lashes which gave the impression that
they were too heavy for his lids.

For many years Bob Lagave had been unaware that this way
he had of looking produced a disturbing effect on others, but
he had now, for some time, been conscious that he possessed the
gift of charm. The natural sweetness of his nature led him to
pretend that he really did feel a desire to please, and so not belie
the promise of his eyes.

He had been a frank and simple-minded boy, rather slow-witted, who felt no surprise that people should respond to him with a smile, or that, at his approach, even the most severe should melt into tenderness. The lazy schoolboy had thought it the most natural thing in the world for the grown-ups to ruffle his hair when he looked at them. Years went by before he managed to build up a personality in keeping with his face, and to exploit, without the slightest hint of ruthlessness, but with a deal of nonchalance and charm, this dangerous gift of his. At long last, he had genuinely fulfilled the promise of his appearance, and had come to be a friendly little dog perpetually asking to be stroked, though the caresses he received were considerably less gentle than those he knew how to give.

Madame Gornac could, no doubt, have learned much about the type merely by paying some attention to the local youths who laboured and sang among the wines, most of whom were, like Bob, much attracted by the girls. The same blood flowed in their veins and his. Through his Lagave grandmother he was closely related to them.

II

"Now I feel too hot."

Bob slightly loosened the enveloping coat which lay round his shoulders, unbuttoned his jacket, and was almost at once conscious again of the cold. His body felt damp. It was as though his young strength were oozing out of him, draining away, and leaving him exhausted.

"It's odd, but my legs seem to give under me."

Elisabeth took hold of a garden chair and dragged it to where Bob was sitting. He dropped into it with a groan: he would never get well, he said: it was all up with him.

She said that it took a long time to get over an attack of pleurisy. Her son Pierre had had to spend two years in the country before he completely regained his strength. She quoted a number of other instances from among her relations. Bob must be patient. But the young man stared at the ground and refused to be comforted. No one, he thought, but he could measure the full extent of the disaster. He had believed in his body. It was the only god he knew. There had been a time when he had never tired of saying to anyone who would listen:

"I don't know what it means to be ill. I don't know what a stomach is. I can eat and drink till all's blue. Even a diet of stones wouldn't bother me: there's nothing I can't digest."

Then, one day, when out for a drive in somebody's car, they had run into a cloudburst between Paris and Versailles. When he got home he had forgotten to change his clothes. To have done so would have shown a lack of confidence in the god, his body. Next morning, while running to catch a motor-bus he had felt a stab of pain in his left side (it was as though some liquid secreted within him had been set moving by the effort he had made). At the time, he had thought it was a stitch, but that evening he went to bed with a temperature.

No going out after that! Being kept in bed had seemed to him more irksome than anything else. He realized then, that, up to the time of his illness, his every effort had been directed to getting back as late as possible to the flat in the rue Vaneau where his parents lived.

"Robert? – Oh, we never see *him*!"

In these words did his mother and father answer all enquiries for their son. It wasn't only the sordid staircase which Bob did his best to keep clear of (there was no service flight) – nor yet the inner courtyard onto which his bedroom looked, where the noise of ashcans being emptied went on all through the night (he could hear up to a late hour returning tenants shouting their names to the concierge, the sound of their retreating footsteps, and the noise of their laughter that oppressed him). It wasn't only the smell with which the tiny kitchen filled this six-thousand-francs a year Paris flat, nor even the enlarged photograph under which Augustin had set an "artistic" bronze, signed "Dalou", representing a Muse on a pedestal offering a laurel wreath to the great man (any great man) whose picture might happen to be suspended above it. He might, perhaps, in course of time, have become blind to the dining-room curtains – chocolate-coloured foliage on a light maroon ground, fringed with bobbles, and to the gilt chairs in the drawing-room, ranged at equal distances round the enormous stuffed, cherry-coloured pouffe engirdled with braid trimmings, on which, each Tuesday, Madame Lagave sat enthroned to "receive" her female callers.

Bob hated the place, but was not so morbidly sensitive as to be unable to put up with it for a few hours. From the moment

of his first being confined to bed, with his mind hovering
within measurable distance of delirium, he had become aware
of his father bending over him three times a day – first thing in
the morning, at noon, and in the evening when he got back
from the office – and had been conscious of a feeling of dread
when he heard the approaching footsteps, of relief when they
died away down the passage, and was forced to admit to himself that it was from Augustin that he had always been in flight,
or, rather, from the contempt he aroused in Augustin's mind,
which was expressed not so much by what he said, as by his
silence when he failed to answer some question put to him by
his son.

Madame Lagave rejoiced to think that she had brought him
up to worship his father. Even as a child he had been taught
that nothing in this wicked world was more worthy of respect
than a man who had succeeded by sheer hard work, who owed
his position to no one but himself. When, in September, he was
taken down for the grape-harvest to stay with his Lagave
grandmother, he lived in terror of the tall, gaunt, hard-faced
old peasant woman who was for ever saying:

"I'm ashamed of him. . . ."

She bore him an unceasing grudge for not having given to
her Augustin something of that happy pride which she had
known on prize-day at the Bordeaux seminary, when, amid the
applause of the assembled multitude, a short-sighted but glori-
ous Augustin had come forward, his arms filled with scarlet
volumes, and his small, pale face held high under its garland
of green pasteboard.

"It's an odd thing" – Augustin said to Maria Lagave; "but as
soon as I saw how fair the brat was, I knew he'd never be a
worker: I had an inkling, even then, that he would be a good-
for-nothing."

The strange thing was that Bob took, physically, after his mother. Like her, he was lean and blond. He had inherited her complexion, the colour of her hair, and the full lips which, though ugly in a woman, seemed to suit the boy. Even his big nose came to him from her. There was nothing of his father in him but the hands and the feet – "so tiny as to be almost shocking" – as the members of his Paris set were never tired of pointing out.

So full of charm had Bob been as a small boy, that Monsieur Lagave had had to give up all idea of submitting him to any drastic form of education. Only on this point had his wife found herself at odds with him. Herself the daughter of a Bordeaux Tax-Collector – the relationship had been flattering to her husband when he had been starting out on his career, though, later, he had had his doubts, and these increased as he rose in the hierarchy – Madame Lagave had thoroughly spoiled the boy when he was a child, in spite of Augustin's protests. Now she could only bow her head when he insisted on "repudiating all responsibility". The boy, it was true, was flabby and unintelligent, but, had he enjoyed the benefit of a stronger hand, might have made some sort of career in the Department of Indirect Taxation. Madame Lagave pleaded in her own defence that Bob's consistently low marks at the Lycée had never cost him the indulgence which was everywhere meted out to him. She reminded her husband how useless had been those visits he had paid to the Vice-Principal for the purpose of urging the latter to "put the screw on".

Against all expectation Bob had succeeded in the School Certificate examination, and Madame Lagave had hoped that this achievement would soften her husband's attitude. He used it, on the contrary, as an excuse for pointing out that the standard must have fallen pretty low if "duds" like Bob could succeed at the first attempt. Severe though Monsieur Lagave was, he was devoid of any gift for self-criticism, and it never occurred to him that the reason of his annoyance might be found in the fact that he had been a bad prophet, that the boy had triumphed in spite of his predictions. Still less would he have been prepared to admit, so entirely was he steeped in self-approbation, so sure was he that he lived in a world far removed from, far above, that of his miserable child, that what he felt was a secret humiliation, a vague jealousy. No more than Maria Lagave, his mother, no more than Jean Gornac, his patron, had he had to struggle against the passions of the heart – and very little against those of the flesh. Even if Jean Gornac had never taken a hand in moulding his future, there can be no doubt that Augustin would have built up for himself an honourable career in the Church. People would have said of him –

"He's not exactly what you would call a mystic, but he is a man of irreproachable life, and an excellent administrator. Men like that are always in demand."

That was certainly true. But neither his mother, Maria, nor old Gornac, both of them as totally unsuited to the passion of love, had been worried by the presence in their lives of a representative of the hostile race – whom those not made to love despise and hate, though they cannot help being jealous of them, or trying, awkwardly, to imitate them. This evening, the pious, strong-charactered Elisabeth Gornac, now not far off fifty, had laid a woman's coat round the young man's shoulders, and that simple gesture had been enough to set the blood pulsing more quickly through her veins. For years now, Augustin Lagave in his eternal black suit (and always with a made-up tie the elastic of which was constantly riding up at the back of his neck) had studied with contemptuous eye the lovely insect with the flickering and spreading wings which had so strangely appeared in his life.

Bob had refused to read Law. He had announced that he was taking a course at the Beaux-Arts, and was working for an interior-decorator. After much bitter arguing, he agreed that his father should enter him as a student of architecture. But that did not put an end to their acrimonious discussions. Some point of disagreement was always sure to come up: to begin with, his first dinner-jacket.

"I never had such a thing when I was your age."

Then, there was the question of a latch-key. Bob, who hated scenes, gave in and beat a retreat. All the same, he never got home until the small hours, and his face, in spite of a pair of puffy eyes, was not that of a young man who had slept under a bridge, or who had seen the sun rise from the Markets. It so happened that, one evening, his father, who had always refused to give him a dress-suit, ran into him in the hall, exquisitely arrayed. He was even wearing a cloak and carrying a stick.

"Where does the money come from? I insist on knowing where the money comes from. It's bad enough to have a good-for-nothing son: I have no intention of letting him bring down dishonour on my head. A thing like this might do you a lot of harm! It would be the last straw if you injured me in my career! (scarcely had this fear taken shape in his mind than it took complete possession of him and made him furious). If you damage my chances of promotion, I shall disown you, have nothing more to do with you! It would be grossly unfair if a long life of hard and honourable work were to be brought to nothing because of the behaviour of a wretched little . . ."

The Renaissance hanging-lamp in the dining-room gave out

a light which was swallowed up by the carved panelling and the curtains with their chocolate floral design.

"Say something, darling!" moaned Madame Lagave. "Give your father an explanation: I'm sure it's all a misunderstanding. . . ."

But the young man leaning against the mantelpiece in his rather too-well-cut dress-suit (the white piqué waistcoat set off the slimness of his figure) hung his head, not from any sense of shame at the suspicions he had aroused, but because he felt embarrassed by the gesticulations of this little man in a black suit who was riding the high horse and shouting.

"At least answer back! Have you got nothing to say? Must you stand there like a mute!"

Bob looked at himself in the glass, smoothed his hair, re-adjusted his cloak, and left the room. He paused on the far side of the door just long enough to say:

"Mother knows all about it. She will tell you that if I go on living here, it's because I don't want to leave *her*, and not because I'm without money. I've made a great deal more this month than you have."

This "exit line" was mere boasting, for Bob was not earning enough to keep himself in pocket-money. Augustin stood for a moment, rooted to the ground with amazement. He looked a question at his wife. But even if Madame Lagave ever really grasped what it was that the young man claimed to be living on, she could never have described it in a way that her husband would have understood. That was why, up to now, she had refused to raise the subject with him, though Bob had begged her to. That there should be people incapable of furnishing their houses for themselves, and idiotic enough to rain gold on a young man just so as to get him to arrange matters in accordance with his own taste, choose their materials and their curtains for them, was something altogether beyond the power of the Lagaves to understand. The truth of the matter was, they just didn't believe it.

Literature is no more meaningless to the illiterate than were problems of colour and form to them. Augustin was always repeating a phrase which old Gornac had heard time and time again:

"Provided I've got good, well-stuffed armchairs . . ."

This he said as a matter of habit, and, in so doing, was slandering himself, since nobody could well have been less sensitive than he was to comfort in any form. If this product of a line of peasants had stayed on at the seminary, this indifference to everything which went by the name of luxury, would have stood him in good stead. He would have been praised for renouncing the sweets of life by which he had never been attracted. He would have been one of those saintly persons whom we somewhat artlessly admire because they have given up, not what they like, but what we like.

That evening, Madame Lagave presented to her husband a number of documents entrusted to her by Bob, letters, estimates and receipts which made it clear that the young man had carried out certain matters of "interior decoration" on commission for two American ladies from New York, and a Roumanian princess. He had also acted as intermediary between a Pole with a Jewish name and a dealer in antique furniture. The honest Civil Servant took comfort in the knowledge that at least one man had figured in these somewhat shady transactions, and that it would be untrue to say that only women could get his son to do a job of work.

Lack of imagination made it impossible for the Lagaves to envisage the kind of life which their son, unknown to them,

was living. He, for his part, had been careful, since the unfortunate incident of the dress-suit, to appear in the rue Vaneau as
seldom as possible. Sometimes, towards evening, they saw him,
like a tired carrier-pigeon, come home to roost, without their
having the faintest idea of the countries over which he had been
flying. They never questioned him, "on principle" Augustin
said, though the truth of the matter was that he had no curiosity
about the doings of others, not even when one of them was his
son. Nothing of importance happened to other people: he was
not interested in other people.

At such times as his father was absent from the drawing-
room, Bob showered attentions and affection on his mother.
But when Augustin came in, he seemed to have lost the use of
his tongue. He sat on the edge of his chair with a blank look in
his eyes, as though Monsieur Lagave, who loved to hold forth
on matters concerned with his work, his chances of promotion,
or politics in general, were speaking in a foreign language. He
found it less easy to put up with stories of examinations and
scholastic triumphs, upon which Monsieur Lagave would
expatiate with stupid satisfaction and intolerable smugness.
But more lurid were his personal recollections – his tales of the
guilty officials he had tracked down, of his skill in smelling
out fraudulent dealings, in sending the defaulters to prison, or
driving them to suicide. The wife and the mother of one of
these had actually knelt at his feet, kissed his hands, and begged
him to show mercy to the wretched creature: a week had been
quite long enough for them to find the sum necessary to make
good the deficit.

"In my work one has to be an ancient Roman. I was
inflexible."

On those evenings Bob went straight from the kitchen,
where he filled a jug with hot water, to his room. The sound

of a bath running momentarily disturbed the game of back-
gammon which, more than anything else, said Monsieur
Lagave, relaxed his mind after a hard day at the Ministry. The
young man did not seek his parents out again. They heard his
door slam. Then Madame Lagave went up to Bob's room
which looked as though a cyclone had struck it, and noticed,
with some annoyance, that he had put yet another shirt for
dirty: he seemed to have no idea how much laundering cost
these days. The water from his bath had splashed all over the
American cloth. It was scarcely worth while to have had the
floor polished that morning. She heard Augustin shout:

"For Heaven's sake, shut that door! I can smell the stuff from
here!"

He loathed scent of every kind, but, especially, the mingled
odour of eau-de-Cologne, chypre and English tobacco which,
for a moment or two, got the better of the whiffs which came
from the kitchen and from the cupboard in the hall where
Monsieur Lagave's clothes were kept.

Once the front-door had shut behind him, Bob was, to all
intents and purposes, lost to them in the empty night – in an
unimaginable vacancy. Had a broomstick carried him off to
some witches' sabbath, the Lagaves could not have been more
incapable of following the turns and twists of his wild ride.
Only when that sudden attack of pleurisy made Bob their
prisoner, did the unknown life which he led so far from them,
flow back to him, since he was no longer able to leave the house.
Those to whom Bob was a source of torment and of joy, worried at having no news of him, flouted the specific injunctions
he had issued, and descended upon the rue Vaneau. From the
very first day of his illness, cars were continually pulling up in
front of the street-door. The concierge was forced to submit
to the humiliation of saying – "there isn't one" when several

ladies started to look for the Lift. One tall young man was so insidiously amiable that Madame Lagave had to open the door of the sickroom a very little way – "just so's I can have a tiny glimpse of Bob". But the patient was so annoyed by this that his temperature reached the highest point, that evening, which it had so far registered. The concierge was instructed to keep the visitors, in future, from coming upstairs, and merely to issue a bulletin of the sufferer's condition. Long confabulations took place in front of the lodge between persons of whom she could say no more than that they did not live in the Quartier.

"One of them was a princess: had a crown on her visiting-card, she did: and then, there was a marquis. . . . Them as he knows is all swells. . . ."

Madame Lagave became so completely bewildered that she found herself already speaking of her son as though he were dead. But she continued to be dazzled. "A flashy lot!" was Augustin's comment, though he was secretly impressed. For the first time the scent of ladies "from the fashionable world", floating round the flat, seemed not to irritate him – either because Bob's illness had made him more tolerant, or because he felt grateful to the young man for the efforts he was making to keep intruders at bay. On this point the invalid was more insistent even than the doctor; no doubt from snobbery, because he was rather ignobly afraid that they would laugh at the chocolate curtains, the enlarged photographs, and, perhaps, even at his parents. But what the indolent young fellow most dreaded was a possible meeting between his father and his friends. Bob was very sensitive, as are all provincials who, acclimatized to the air of Paris, have taken root in a very different world from the one in which they were brought up, to the different climate of the city. Exposed to the "special language"

of the Smart Set, a man like Augustin Lagave would at first
have been completely at sea, and, after the initial strangeness
had worn off, would have become exasperated.

Even when convalescent, the young man still, for a few days
more, put up a show of resistance. But already, heralding the
invasion by friends who would not take no for an answer, their
flowers filled every available vase, drenching the rooms with a
scent which is usually associated with weddings. A box from
Boissier's, sent by the princess, stood on a ridiculous sham-
Beauvais table, where it looked as much out of place as the
princess herself would have done perched on the cherry-
coloured pouffe in the drawing-room.

When Bob's temperature returned to normal, Monsieur
Lagave's mood began to change for the worse. It infuriated him
that his wife should be impressed by all the preserved fruit and
flowers. Her admiration of Bob was just as blind as in the days
when she had declared that he "would win a prize in any baby-
contest" (though even then Augustin had had a foreboding
that the beautiful infant, so different from himself, would turn
out a failure).

Every evening, when the respectable Civil Servant got home,
he began his usual grumble:

"Place stinks like a bawdy-house!"

Then, to cleanse the air, he would throw all the windows
open, though the Spring, that year, was cold and rainy.

One Saturday morning, when he happened to have come
home earlier than usual, a young woman was just emerging
from Bob's room. At sight of him she sped through the open
door like a frightened bird. Augustin had just time to notice
two sultry eyes under the brim of a small felt hat pulled low
over her forehead, two long legs, and a pair of slim feet in

shark-skin shoes. He leaned over the balcony and watched this unknown female get into a saloon car, take the wheel and start the engine: – one of those women, no doubt, who always look as though they had nothing on under their abbreviated skirts, drive their own cars, and visit young men in their own homes! Determined to make a scene, Monsieur Lagave opened the door of his son's room, and saw him stretched on the bed with his head in the pillow and his eyes half-shut. He remained for a moment uncertain what to do, then, closing the door, went into his study, sat down at his desk, and began to annotate a Report. He refrained from mentioning the incident to Madame Lagave when she came in. Not for the world would this product of a line of peasant forbears have so far lowered himself as to start a discussion with a wife who had passed over into the enemy camp! Ever since Bob had been taken ill, she had watched over the boy like a broody old hen, with the same doting look in her eyes as when he had been a small child, and Augustin complained that he was not occupying in his own home the position – the one and only position which was due to him – of head of the family. Though he had succeeded, gradually, in his attempts to persuade her of their son's uselessness, though he had made of her a proud wife but a humiliated mother, it was the mother now who was raising her head, taking her revenge, finding in her child a value which, though it in no way recalled what she admired in her husband, seemed to her scarcely less precious, and, what was even more important, brought contentment to her pride.

How could Monsieur Lagave have known that it was she who, in his absence, had thrown open the house to the invaders? – to this young woman, first and foremost, a young woman of genuine fashion, a Mademoiselle de la Sesque, related to the la Sesques of Bazas, the only visitor whom Bob was glad to see, the only one of them all he had introduced to his mother? The others came only in the afternoons, and Madame Lagave was under strict orders not to show herself to them. But, from the next-door room she could hear them laughing, could smell the smoke of their cigarettes. Through the key-hole, or through the half-open door when the maid took in tea, she got a glimpse of them seated in a circle round Bob's bed: the princess, another fair-haired woman, a lanky young man who looked like a crane, with a head too small for his body, and shoulders like those of an Egyptian wall painting, and, the Polish Jew with crinkly hair and a pendent lower lip. These comprised the "faithful", but other, less intimate, visitors frequently joined them. A general air of youth made them all look alike: young men, youngish women in their forties, all of them gazing in the same besotted way at a Bob who seemed a complete stranger to his mother – aggressive, obstinate and insolent. They laughed at his lightest word. Madame Lagave could never have believed that her darling could be so witty. She scarcely recognized his voice, so different was this Bob from the taciturn youth who sat at the family table. It was difficult to believe that these smart folk admired him to the extent they seemed to do. There must be something quite extraordinary about him, thought Madame Lagave, for people who were so hard to please thus to devour him with their eyes. She did not know that what they loved so passionately in him was their own tarnished youth, now at its last gasp, or already dead, everything which they had lost for ever and could now dotingly see reflected in this young crea-ture's ephemeral bloom. It was in some sort a religion which brought them to his bedside, a mystery of which they were the initiates, with its rites, its sacred formulae, its liturgy. Nothing had any value in their eyes but this charm which nothing could replace, which was lost to them for ever. So, there they were, seated in a circle round a supine body which, still for a short time, would burn with the fires of youth. Illness had changed scarcely anything in his appearance, but it made them more fully realize how fragile, how fugitive his charm was. Perhaps Bob felt that, for them, he was no more than a halting-place where the god whom all these fanatics adored, was taking a short rest. Perhaps he may have known that it was not to him – a man without birth, money, talent or intelligence, that their worship was addressed. Maybe this knowledge was the reason for the ill-temper with which he rebuffed their praise, for his capricious-ness of mood, as of a boy-Caesar, with which he treated them. How arrogantly he made them do his bidding!

One day, when the Polish Jew had been profuse in his apologies for not having succeeded in finding anywhere the grape-fruit which Bob was so eager to sample, the young man had had the effrontery to make him go down four flights of stairs, with instructions not to show his face again without the fruit about which he was so curious.

It had been rather late before the foreigner returned, and the others had sat there rather longer than usual, waiting for him. Madame Lagave was hanging about on the other side of the door, terrified at the thought that, at any moment now, her husband might come back. For the last few days, his mood had been such, that he might quite easily fling the whole lot of them into the street. Bob shared her anxiety, and she could hear him urging and bullying them to go.

It was not in the flat, but on the staircase, that Monsieur Lagave ran into them. He had to stand back against the wall for the crowd of young men and painted women with high voices, who stared him out of countenance, and then burst out laugh-ing, to pass. When the model State-employé reached his land-ing, he leaned over the banister for a few moments, and listened. For once he had no difficulty in understanding their private language.

"*Could* that have been the father?"

"Did you see the father, princess? he's really something beyond belief!"

"Too utterly incredible!"

"Just like one of those bacteria you see under a microscope, magnified a thousand times!"

"I never really knew people like that existed. One doesn't as a rule see them in a state of freedom: they spend most of their time behind bars, lurking between piles of dusty paper. . . ."

"I was prepared for anything, but not, I confess, for a little misshapen dwarf like that!"

"It really is beyond belief: all the same, I'm glad to have seen it!"

"Rather shattering, all the same. Something of Père Ubu about him, don't you think, princess?"

"If you squelched him there'd be just a black mess. I expect he's got ink in his veins!"

"Did you hear what Jean said? – that if you trod on him he'd bleed ink?"

"I don't honestly think it can be the father: our Bob couldn't have been produced by *that*."

"A love-lorn cockroach in the act – that makes you think, doesn't it, princess?"

"Stop it, Alain!"

By this time they had reached the street. But the wretched little man, bent double over the banisters, looking like a broken doll, could still hear their laughter.

Monsieur Lagave's key turned in the lock. While his wife and son were breathing more freely now that the danger (so they thought) had been averted, he went to his room. Planted in front of the looking-glass, with his short legs slightly straddled, he looked at his reflection for a long time, and felt pleased by what he saw. He straightened his made-up tie, settled his pince-nez on his nose, flicked a few specks from the collar of his coat, raised himself on his toes as he did each time he went in to see his chief, and summoned his wife. With his fingers between two buttons of his waistcoat, he told her that he had rung the doctor, that Bob could now be moved and ought to have a change of air, that the sooner he went, the better. His grand-mother Lagave would expect him in two days' time. Caught unawares, Madame Lagave stammered out that princess R . . . had invited Bob to convalesce in her villa at Cannes, and that Bob had accepted. Augustin turned on his wife that dead look which always reduced her to a state of helpless embarrassment, and repeated his sentence of banishment. Bob would catch the evening train next day: his mother would go with him as far as Langon, and return to Paris at once. The concierge and her husband had already received instructions to turn away the pack of swindlers and tarts brought by his wretched son, people they had thoughtlessly admitted to the home of a man with an un-sullied reputation.

"I don't want to hear another word on the subject!"

When Madame Lagave went into her son's room to deliver the paternal message, he was lying on his bed with his eyes shut and his arms at his sides. He had not touched the grape-fruit which, on the white plate, looked like the fruits of Canaan. Smoke was still rising from little piles of cigarette-stubs. The window which looked onto the gloomy courtyard was open, and framed a patch of sky – a June sky of unsullied brightness triumphing over the city's soot and dust. She was stunned at the ease with which her boy gave up the prospect of a holiday in a villa owned by a princess.

"This is a much better arrangement: I can't stand those people!"

"That's not nice of you, Bob: they've been so kind!"

"They're just the bottom, mother: Society hacks, and nothing else."

He was looking at her through half-closed lids.

"Papa is right . . . they make me sick!"

How bitter his voice sounded! With his elbow on the pillow and his head in his hand, he looked suddenly much older. On the mortal melancholy of his face only a shadow of youth and freshness now showed. All of a sudden, he smiled at his mother, and said:

"She's going to be at Arcachon in July . . . we could quite easily meet. It's fifty miles from Viridis, but she'll have her car."

"Can you really see Mademoiselle de la Sesque in your grandmother's house? . . . You must be mad, my poor boy, to think of such a thing!"

Oh, they'd meet right enough! What happiness there was in the thought that she would be living and breathing, in the same part of the country, and not so very far from him.

III

THAT evening, on the terrace at Viridis, Bob Lagave, pointing to the horizon, put a question to Elisabeth Gornac, not for the first time.

"Arcachon lies somewhere in that direction, doesn't it?"

She was surprised that he should be so insistent.

"What's so interesting about Arcachon?"

He answered in a low voice, as though he wanted to prick her curiosity:

"Somebody."

Madame Gornac's silence disappointed him. He would have liked her to press him for an explanation. She, however, said nothing, and he went on:

"A girl."

Madame Gornac nodded her head, smiled, but maintained a tactful silence. She asked none of the questions which Bob was expecting. Yet another evening would pass before, after moving from confidence to confidence, he would be able to pluck up sufficient courage to ask to be allowed to bring her to Viridis. Paula de la Sesque could easily make the trip from Arcachon and back in the same day, by car. But it was utterly impossible that she should cross the threshold of Maria Lagave's house. This terrace was the only place where they could meet. He would have to tell Elisabeth a great deal about Paula before she would consent. Would a lady, living in the country and completely out of touch with modern ways, dream for a single moment that a young woman could possibly be allowed to drive over sixty miles alone in a car for the sole purpose of spending a day with a young man? Bob would have abandoned

36

the project in despair had it not been for the fact that the la Sesque family was very well known round Bazas. One of them had been a Minister of State under the Empire. Half ruined by the revolution of the fourth of September, they had sold their farms (Jean Gornac had bought several) and settled in Paris. Bob wanted to persuade himself that Elisabeth Gornac would feel flattered at the idea of offering hospitality to the young woman in question. But would so pious a person allow herself to be mixed up in a love-affair?

'Unless, of course, I can make her believe that we are engaged. . . .'

But that must wait for the time being. Down in the plain the six o'clock express was rumbling over the viaduct.

"It's getting cold. Time to go home, dear boy. Your grandmother will scold you."

It was true that Maria Lagave could not bear meals to be kept waiting even for a minute. Only in Elisabeth's company could Bob breathe freely in this out of the way spot. The poisonous atmosphere of adoration which his Paris friends provided had become more necessary to him than he knew. To say that his charm had no effect upon his grandmother would be an understatement: everything about him got on the old woman's nerves – his ties, his silk shirts, his white flannel trousers. At night he had to wait until this daughter of the soil was in bed before unfastening the safety-pin with which she kept the curtains of the sleeping-recess tightly closed, "so's the young caution shan't feel the air". Only then did he dare throw off the enormous stuffed eiderdown which she insisted he should keep on his bed all night – to make sure he'd get a "proper sweat". But the worst of his misdoings was opening the window, a piece of rashness which, in the eyes of Maria Lagave, was tantamount to committing suicide. But the care and cossetting with which she surrounded him did not, for a moment, take Bob in: it concealed no warmth of affection.

"Your dad put you in my care, and I accepted the responsibility: besides, he's the one as pays. When you get back to Paris, you'll be at liberty to ruin your health without nobody interfering. But *I* give the orders here."

Her eyes were like those of an angry hen, and he stood in mortal fear of them. If he asked for hot water for a bath, or complained that the cuffs of his shirt were not ironed flat, they had an uncomfortable way of looking him over from head to feet.

"Your father has always worn'em round."

Then there was his mania for always changing his linen.

"It's not work as makes you dirty! . . . Why can't you wait till next washing-day? Don't suppose you know what laundering costs. . . ."

Elisabeth Gornac watched him hobbling away. She kept her eyes fixed on the object of her loving concern until he disappeared in the shade cast by the tall trees in the alley. Then she looked across to the point on the horizon at which he had been so ardently gazing. 'A young girl . . .' she thought. Not that the heart of this placid woman was in the least disturbed. It was time for her to go back to Monsieur Gornac who was probably already grumbling at being neglected . . . besides, there was her son Pierre's room to be got ready. He never gave the slightest indication of when he might be expected to turn up. Very soon now he would be arriving. She earnestly hoped that they would manage to get through the few weeks of his holiday without a quarrel. She registered a silent vow to avoid any sort of a clash. She would make a real effort not to irritate him, would even go so far, if necessary, as to pretend to agree with his views. But it never took Pierre long to get on the wrong

side of his grandfather! The gulf between Monsieur Gornac and
his grandson could scarcely have been wider! It was difficult to
believe that they were of the same blood: Pierre, so deeply
religious, almost a mystic, for ever "dreaming", as the old man
put it – so wholly detached from the things of this world, from
money – almost a socialist (would you believe it!), always
buried in some book or other, or making lecture tours of the
Paris slums and the provincial cities. The closer Elisabeth got to
the house, the more clearly could she envisage what their next
meeting would be like: the old man in his most provocative
mood, Pierre producing paradoxes, high words and slammed
doors. Strange though it might seem, it was she, so pious by
nature, who inevitably took Monsieur Gornac's side in controversy. She almost always found herself at variance with her
son. Their shared faith had no power to bring them together;
but with the old radical she could rub along very comfortably.

From the moment of their first meeting, Monsieur Gornac
had thought of her as a woman after his own heart. She was a
"countrywoman born" – by which he did not mean a sunburned amazon trained to hard physical exercise. A countrywoman, when she was also a lady, meant somebody who lived
shut away in her house, scarcely ever leaving her sitting-room
or one of her kitchens: somebody who never went out bare-
headed, who would never venture, even into the garden, without gloves. The idea of walking would be anathema to such
a person. Plump perhaps, but that would be because she drove
everywhere. Only in shadowed, downstairs rooms could her
pendulous cheeks have become so white.

Elisabeth, however, had, in her own way, led an active
existence. Her father, Hector Lavignasse, had been ruined by the
phylloxera, but had restored his diminished fortune thanks to a

turpentine factory which he could never have run successfully if his daughter had not helped him. She was a marvel at administration and book-keeping.

When she became Madame Prudent Gornac, her father-in-law at once struck up a close relationship with her because he found that he could associate her with all his ventures. He found in his daughter-in-law the very qualities which he knew that he lacked, for, as frequently happens, this man of business was a poor administrator. So entirely was his mind taken up by the purchase of land and by politics, that he had little time to give to the running of his house-property and his estates, the number of which increased year by year. His two sons (and this had been the great disappointment of his life) were no manner of use to him. To say nothing of the younger, the "wanting" one, who had gone off to Paris to paint, and been brought back in his coffin, though nobody in the neighbourhood knew exactly why, or how, he had died – Prudent, the elder, who was the "very picture of his poor mother . . . a Péloueyre, every inch of him", had shown in business matters a lack of interest that was really almost criminal – and the same could be said, much to old Gornac's grief, of his grandson, Pierre.

Prudent, on the ground of his having to keep an eye on the forest land, lived on his farm at Le Bos, where he was looked after by the farmer's wife. He didn't even go out shooting, but was for ever "glued to his books". He had done well at school, and, according to the curé, was intelligent. But, "a precious lot of good that'll do him", thought his father. So absurdly shy as to be almost uncouth, his health undermined by aperitifs and white wine, young Gornac had the reputation of being an unlicked cub in a district rich in such boors. But that was not all. Ruled in everything by his father, he had scarcely, if at all, broken free of the old man's domination, not even when he

married Mademoiselle Elisabeth Lavignasse. It had been left to
the elder Gornac to buy the furniture, supervise the structural
improvements and engage the servants. Prudent had thought it
quite natural that his father should cut all the wood he needed,
without a word to him, though the pine forests had been left to
him by his mother.

He had, however, shown signs of jibbing when Monsieur
Garnac started to summon Elisabeth to Viridis or Bordeaux,
and to keep her there for days on end. Quite often, business was
a mere pretext. For the first time in his life the old man could
now discuss matters which interested him with a member of the
family. Elisabeth loved the land, and would gladly have spent
her life in organizing Monsieur Gornac's acquisitions. But she
was a woman of sense, devoted to her husband, and gifted with
a strong sense of duty. After one year of marriage Prudent had
given up the four aperitifs a day which was the normal ration
of his neighbours: sometimes he even took a bath, and he now
shaved almost every morning.

Since Elisabeth had a way of remaining deaf to her father-in-
law's appeals, it was he, now, who turned up, unannounced, at
Le Bos. Even before the trap had turned into the road leading
to the farm, Prudent could recognize the familiar tinkle of the
horse-bells, the cracking of the paternal whip. His heart went
into his throat: good-bye to happiness! It did not worry him in
the least to see his father taking the end of the table, behaving
like the master of the house, bullying the farmers, imposing on
the household the food of his choice, his fads, his hours of rising
and of going to bed. But he did resent the look of happy surprise
on Elisabeth's face. She, who talked so little with her husband,
found endless subjects about which to question her father-in-
law. If Prudent shyly tried to take part in the conversation, she
said to him:

"These are matters you know nothing about."

It would have been not the slightest use for her to attempt an explanation. The poor young man's mind was a blank where estate business was concerned. His father had no patience with him.

"You're never informed about anything!"

"But I didn't know . . . you never told me. . . ."

"It's only you who are so ignorant: other people manage to find out about these things. I don't have to go into a lot of detail with Elisabeth."

Domestics and farmers had got into the habit of never dealing with anybody but Madame, and when they spoke of "Moussu" or "Moussu Gornac", it was never Prudent they meant, but his father.

During her pregnancies, Elisabeth did not move from the house, and Le Bos became old Gornac's home-port. He took his account-books there, and Elisabeth was only too glad to audit them, which she could do without leaving her room. She managed everything by dint of writing endless letters.

"Ah, my dear!" sighed her father-in-law, "what a pity it is I'm not in Prudent's shoes. You and I together could have done wonders!"

She protested that nothing in the world would have induced her to marry such an old heathen. All the same, it was religion that held them together, though religion of a different kind – the pines, the grapes, in short, the land. The love they had in common was their Communion. If their hearts could have been laid bare, there would have been found, inscribed upon them, the names of all the farms, both great and small, the possession of which was their perpetual joy, and a source of strength to them when they had to face set-backs in business and deaths in the family. It prevented any tragedy from spoiling their rich delight in the flavour of life. A fortnight after the death of his second son, Jean Gornac bought, "for a song", some vineyards which abutted on Viridis. Elisabeth, after the loss of her two babies, took a slightly longer time before returning to her ledgers and talking business with the farmers: all the same, it was interest in the estate that first re-awakened in her the will to live.

"I know that we can't take our possessions with us into the grave, Monsieur le Curé" – she said: "but they stay on after us, all the same."

To her husband she once remarked:

"I sometimes wonder how you manage not to be bored: what'd become of me here, if I hadn't got the land to attend to, I don't know."

Prudent dared not answer: "You give me everything I want ..." for such affectionate exchanges were not current in the Gornac family. He loved his fields and his forests because, but for them, he would never have succeeded in marrying Elisabeth: but he was jealous of them. It hurt him, when emotion left him tongue-tied in the night, to hear Elisabeth's voice saying in the nuptial darkness:

"Remind me to-morrow morning to get you to sign the Lalanne lease."

She was quite convinced that if only she had not left her husband alone on the fatal October day when she had had to go over to Viridis to superintend the grape-harvest, he would not have died. He never indulged to excess when she was with him but, when he was left on his own, he got drunk every day. No doubt about it, if he had been sober, he would not have fallen so clumsily from the trap, would not have cracked his skull. She often thought back to that occurrence with bitter regret, though without a shadow of remorse. She had done what it had been her duty to do. There had been a strike among the hands, and, when things were at their worst, old Gornac had been struck down with rheumatism. The crop that year had been superb, but there had been a shortage of casks, and the grapes couldn't be left to rot. The white could wait, but for the red it would have spelled disaster. She had responded to her father-in-law's first cry for help, and had saved the situation. She had had no time even to answer Prudent's letters. The poor fellow had quite failed to realize the seriousness of what was happening. A crop, the like of which one doesn't see once in ten years, was in peril. To that he attached no importance. The only thing he really loved was peace and comfort.

Many and many a time did she recall the telegram which had been delivered to her at Viridis: "serious accident Prudent condition desperate. . . ." The victoria had been got ready in haste, and into it she had climbed with her father-in-law who was still crippled with the rheumatism. She had cried a good deal in the privacy of the lowered hood. Would she arrive in time to close his eyes? Had he seen a priest? Monsieur Gornac tried to reconstruct the accident:

"This is what must have happened. . . ."

His mind had to have something concrete to work on. Now and again his attention wandered:

"Did you write to Lavergne about the casks? . . ."

"Of course I did, father: don't worry."

With a great effort he brought his mind back to his son, now at death's door. He was profoundly grieved. This was a matter affecting the family. Both his children had preceded him to the grave: only a grandson survived who took no interest in the land. His feeling at that moment was of the kind he had always found intolerable: an important piece of business had been badly handled: he was going to be involved in a loss: there was nothing he could do about it. Prudent Gornac, as an individual, might disappear without being much missed: but the death of the last of the Gornac sons was a disaster. Still, why think about what he would leave behind him when his turn came? He was only seventy-one, and his father had lived to be eighty-four. . . . He would have his daughter-in-law to himself.

'That is, if she doesn't marry again. . . .'

"It'd be the last straw!" – he muttered.

"What did you say, father?"

"Nothing, my dear, nothing . . . we're getting near Le Bos."

But already, in his mind, he was drawing up a Will in favour of his daughter-in-law, provided she did not re-marry.

His thoughts turned again to Prudent. He tried to imagine the corpse, made an effort to feel as he ought to feel about a dead son. Seated there beside him, Elisabeth, too, was patiently endeavouring to bring her mind back from where it was wandering far from her perfectly sincere grief. She thought about her life, about what her life was going to be now: a new situation, a new life. . . . Her son, Pierre, was twelve years old. What rights had she as a widow? They had held in common only such property as might be acquired after marriage. But there had been none. Didn't she remember having heard that a widow was entitled to a fixed percentage of her husband's estate over and above her share in their common holdings? But what, precisely, did that amount to? She would have to wait before discussing the question with her father-in-law. Pierre, when he came of age, would not be interested in money matters: fundamentally, he was just such another as poor Prudent. Poor Prudent! – she must say a prayer for him. She had forgotten her rosary: her fingers would have to do instead – in that way she would keep her thoughts from wandering.

When the victoria turned in under the Le Bos oaks, Elisabeth

became sharply conscious of her grief. One of the farmers suddenly materialized out of the darkness, jumped on the running-
board, and proceeded to give a description of the accident,
in a strong country brogue. The poor "Moussu" was still
breathing.

Did he recognize her? The eyes he turned on her were
vacant. But the curé was sure he did:

"He understood what I was saying to him: he pressed my
hand. . . ."

IV

B ᴜᴛ, ten years later, this same, strong-minded woman, this "business-woman" as old Gornac called her, was here, on the terrace at Viridis, standing where young Lagave had recently been lying, her elbow on the balustrade. She felt no eagerness to know precisely how far the last sulphate spraying had got, nor whether the engine had been put to rights. She was thinking of the girl with whom Bob was in love. Down below, in the plain, a train was crawling across the viaduct, the evening train which very soon now would bring her son to Viridis. Had Pierre ever been in love?... had anyone ever been in love with him?

"He's got his head screwed on," she had got into the habit of saying: "we needn't feel any anxiety about him: he'll never do anything foolish. He has strong principles, perhaps a little too strong. His natural instinct is to give: he is over-generous, or, rather, it would be truer to say that he doesn't know what it means to have to make money: what he has, has never, so to speak, cost him a penny. He is completely ignorant of the value of money. . . ."

Elisabeth remembered this evening how, the year before, he had refused an invitation to a dance at the nearby château of Malromé, and how she had pressed him to go, saying that he was no better than a boor, a wild-man-of-the-woods, and how he had replied:

"I'm such a bad dancer: besides, young women find me a crashing bore. They think I'm too serious: they only like playboys. . . ."

That had made Elisabeth lose her temper:

47

"Which of them do you want?" she had replied: "you've only got to raise a finger and she's yours. . . . You're a *catch*!"

Would she use those words to him now? She was suddenly conscious of a ridiculous feeling, a feeling of humiliation because Pierre had no success with women, because women didn't like him. Would she have felt flattered if he had been, like young Lagave, trailed by all and sundry, endlessly pursued?

She went back by way of the tree-lined alley, and knocked at the door of the Galberts' cottage. They had just finished their supper and rose to their feet as she entered. Only the vines on the lower slope remained to be sprayed. The oxen would have to be given a rest to-morrow. The Italian whom Galbert had taken on worked like a horse. The vines needed water. A bit of a storm would do the job. That was all very well, but when one prayed for rain, one got hail!

"The la Sesque girl! – so that's who it is!"

"Don't tell me you know her?"

The face which Bob Lagave turned to Elisabeth seemed suddenly all lit up, blazing. He was sitting on the edge of the terrace, with his legs dangling. Elisabeth Gornac was standing beside him. It was ten o'clock: there was a quiver in the early mist.

"The last time I saw her, she was in her nurse's arms. Her mother and I were quite intimate. As a matter of fact, we are cousins . . . exactly how, I can't tell you . . . but we are, and closely related: the great-grandmother of your young woman was my grandfather's half-sister. You see, one of the la Sesques married twice, and his second wife was a Lavignasse. His first was a Péloueyre, so we're related on that side, too, through my mother-in-law. . . . My poor Bob, how I must be boring you. . . ."

She certainly was not doing that! . . . Paula would be free
to come here! He would see her!

"Then since you're on such very close terms with her mother
. . ."

"Very close terms – how you do jump to conclusions! I
suppose you know that the la Sesques are ruined? They sold
their land at the worst possible moment. My father-in-law
bought La Farrière for next to nothing. And then, you see, they
moved to Paris. I sometimes wonder how they're getting on.
I've never seen such clothes as those women had! Some say
that they are living on capital. Maybe they are, but capital
doesn't last for ever. I'm not setting up to pass judgment on
anybody, but I don't much like that sort of thing. They're
bohemians, the artist type, certainly not our sort."

"All the same, if Paula de la Sesque's car had a breakdown
somewhere near here, you'd think it quite natural, wouldn't
you, to offer her hospitality while it was being put right?"

"Why, of course . . ."

"Good – and suppose I told you that she will have a breakdown at your very gates, one of these days? . . ."

He was trying to catch Elisabeth Gornac's eye. There was
a wheedling expression on his face. She blushed furiously, and
broke in on him:

"I can see what you're going to say, and my answer is – no.
I have no wish to get mixed up in your casual affairs."

He protested that this was no common intrigue, that Paula
and he regarded themselves as engaged.

"What! you engaged to Mademoiselle de la Sesque?"

She laughed. Her laughter was too loud, and went on for too
long. Bob compressed his lips and half closed his eyes, as he did
when he was afraid of showing that he was hurt. His voice, too,
grew softer, a sure sign that he was holding his anger in check.

"The la Sesques, don't you see, have adopted Paris ways: don't make any mistake about that. To Society folk in Paris, you, I, and the la Sesques are all of a piece ... with this difference, that I am invited to houses where the la Sesques could never so much as show the tips of their noses. ..."

He could hold himself in no longer. Since his illness, he was no longer in control of his nerves. ... It worried Elisabeth to think that she had upset him: all she was concerned about was his health.

"There's no need to be insolent. You have completely failed to take my meaning. When I said that I couldn't imagine your being engaged, it was only because you're so young."

Bob made a great effort to keep calm.

"When I told you that we are engaged, I didn't intend you to understand that I've spoken to her parents. ... They know nothing about it. They'd be furious if they did. Naturally, they want her to marry money. But look here, when you see Paula you'll realize why I asked you to help me in this way. ... She's not like other girls. ... She couldn't do anything wrong if she tried. ..."

"Wait a moment ... yes, I remember now ... it was Pierre who spoke with such admiration of Paula de la Sesque. ... He met her at a pic-nic, last year: at last, he said, I've found a young woman to whom one can talk! ..."

"It's quite true that one can talk to her, even when one's as learned as Pierre must be. How is Pierre, by the way? ... I've scarcely set eyes on him since we used to play together here, as kids: – just caught sight of him once, last year, and that's all. ... But even when he was twelve, don't you remember? he always went about with a book in his pocket."

"Yes, in those ways he's the true son of his father, who never went out, for no matter how short a walk, without some book or other. . . . I'm expecting him any day now. . . . He has a perfect mania for never letting me know when he's coming."

"What seems to me so extraordinary, madame, is that any-one like Paula could so much as look at me. . . . No, don't laugh. I swear to you that there's no intimacy between us. When you see her you'll understand what I mean. . . ."

"Still, I suppose you do exchange kisses sometimes? Come on, admit it: am I right?"

Elisabeth was fanning herself with her handkerchief.

Very simply he replied:

"I kiss her forehead, her hair, her eyes, her hand . . ."

"What more can you want? . . ."

He stared in astonishment. How could any one be so un-ruffled? His laughter, when it came, sounded faintly common.

"That's all *you* know," he muttered: "but let me tell you this: you won't find anywhere another woman like Paula de la Sesque: I certainly haven't."

"That may be true of Paris. We, here, in the provinces . . ."

"The local beauties? – Oh, save me from them!" – he laughed again in the same rather vulgar way. "I know what I'm talking about, madame; there is no one like Paula, you can take my word for that."

He swung his legs, and gazed into the distance. Elisabeth averted her eyes. Suddenly, she gave in to her longing to make him happy.

"Have it your own way! I shall be only too glad to have her here: but only for a day or two, mind: just long enough for her to get the car mended."

"You'll really do that?"

"It's very wrong of me. . . ."

He jumped to his feet, and kissed Madame Gornac's hands: "I'll write at once, and take the letter into Langon, so as not to miss the evening post!"

He made off. Elisabeth called after him:

"Don't run . . . you'll work yourself into a sweat! . . ."

But he was too far away to hear. His grandmother's house was as cold as a cellar: he'd almost certainly catch a chill. She had done wrong to let him extract that promise. Still, she was running no risk. But what would her father-in-law say if he knew that she was encouraging the stratagems of young love?

'It's not really a bit like me: I was too weak with the boy.'

Ought she to tell her confessor what she had done? Bob had given her his word that there was nothing anyone could object to.

'But the la Sesques would hold me guilty; and quite rightly, too. . . . I realize that such a marriage would be looked on by them as nothing short of a disaster. . . . Their daughter dragged down. . . . The young people with nothing to live on. . . .'

As she made her way back along the alley, preoccupied with her thoughts, and her eyes on the ground, she saw a scarf which Bob had dropped in his hurry. She picked it up. The boy must have found it in one of his grandmother's wardrobes, but, round his neck, the peasant object looked as though it had come straight from Barclay's. It smelt of tobacco and ambergris. She put it in her work-bag. Just as she was passing the Galberts' cottage, she caught sight of Monsieur Gornac standing by the open door. He had lifted a corner of the tattered material which half hid the entrance. The Galberts were eating their dinner. It was just like him to give them no rest! It never occurred to him that his work-people might have other things than his interests to think about. She called to him. There was a note of irritation in her voice.

"Oh do, for Heaven's sake, let them eat in peace! Besides, it's time you came up to the house, father! our own meal will be ready."

He leaned on her arm, grumbling as he walked: she had forgotten to tell the Galberts that because of the heat siesta time would be prolonged until four, and that the men must go on working after sundown. She was not listening to him. Her mind was filled with young Lagave's concerns. She ought not to have consented . . . a woman of her age! She admitted that Monsieur Gornac had been perfectly right. As they entered the dining-room, he had said:

"Your mind's all over the place, my dear."

It was quite true: she didn't seem able to concentrate on anything; it was time she took a hold on herself. After lunch she would go across the road to Maria's and warn Bob not to count on her. But wouldn't the old woman think her visit rather odd?

'I'll say I came to bring back the scarf which Bob dropped.'

"Madame Prudent!—and in this heat, too!"

Maria Lagave stared at Elisabeth's scarlet face. The kitchen was cool and dark. Flies were buzzing, and struggling in their death-agony on strips of sticky paper.

"It's so hot they can't even take the oxen out. It's only Robert goes gallivanting at this time of day."

"Is he not here? I've brought back this scarf of his. . . ."

"It's really most kind of you. . . . Fancy putting yourself about for that young scamp under such a blazing sun! **You**

could have waited till the next time he went to see you: he's
always pestering you: you've no consideration, I tell him."

The old woman did not look up from her knitting. Elisabeth
wondered what she was thinking.

"It's as hot inside our house as it is out. Besides, I have been
sitting down all morning: it does me good to have a walk. You
don't mean to say he's tramping the road on a day like this?"

"Something about an urgent letter, he said. Nonsense, I call
it! As though the letters of a young fellow who's never done a
hand's turn in his life couldn't wait! But oh no! – it had got to
go this evening at all costs. He's as lazy a creature as ever was
seen, and wouldn't get out of his chair to pick up my scissors –
but off he goes to Langon on his bicycle! I refused point blank
to run the risk of the horse getting sunstroke: horses cost a
pretty penny now. You can take my word for it, when our
fine gentleman wants something bad enough, there's no more
talk of his being tired! You should have seen him! Something
bad to do with a woman, I'll be bound!"

"You know what young men are, Maria. . . ."

"Indeed I do! but there's some as takes their fun and does a bit
of work, too. There's a time and a place for all things. But this
young fellow's a no-good, if not worse. His poor father didn't
deserve a son like that, he didn't! Like father like son, indeed –
that's just a pack o'nonsense, Madame Prudent!"

Elisabeth plunged into the furnace of the open air, and crossed
the deserted road. Every living thing had gone to ground.

"Well, the wine's drawn . . ." she muttered: "there's nothing
I can do about it. . . ."

After all, it wasn't a very serious matter. The la Sesque girl
was old enough to take care of herself. All the same, this was
the last time she'd meddle in his affairs, and she'd tell him as

much. What if Pierre happened to be at Viridis when that precious car "broke down" . . . of course, he'd believe that the accident was genuine . . . he wasn't so nasty-minded as to think anything else. . . . She went and lay down in the shuttered drawing-room. She could hear old Gornac snoring away upstairs. The sun had cast a spell over the world and left it dazed. It reigned unchallenged in the heavens. Not even a cock crowed. Only lovers were taking advantage of the universal torpor. Down among the drowsing vines, in the coolness of the wine-store, hands were feeling for hands, and faces with eyes closed, coming together. Until four o'clock the world would be empty, a welcome place for those who had no dread of fire. What should they fear? This heat only intensified their own. The cracked soil was no hotter than their bodies. Elisabeth Gornac fell asleep.

V

I T was three days later, at the same hour, when the heat of the day was at its fiercest, that Bob opened the front-door, and a young woman's voice could be heard answering his. Elisabeth got up and, at a single glance, took in the couple standing in the drawing-room doorway. She watched Paula as she removed her light dust-coat, to reveal a sturdy body dressed for tennis. It gave her something of a shock, when the girl took off her hat, to see how like a boy's, a good-looking boy's was the tanned face with its short brown hair. She started to speak, breathlessly, as shy persons do. She asked the charming creature for news of her parents. Life in the country, she said, must be rather boring for her, after Paris ... there weren't many distractions at Viridis. Then, noticing that neither of the young people even made an effort to reply, she cut short her flow of conversation. Paula took the opportunity of thanking her for having shown such trust in her, and assured her that she would not have to repent of having done so. With a self-conscious laugh, Elisabeth asked whether the break-down would be put right by nightfall. It was Bob who answered that Mademoiselle de la Sesque expected to be able to start for home late the following afternoon.

"We're going to dine this evening at the hotel in Langon. We thought it would be better, because of Monsieur Gornac."

"Then I'll have your room ready ... would you like to go upstairs now? ... Oh, but I see you don't need to change: you've got a light frock on already. I'll leave you two together: you must have a lot to talk about. You can have the drawing-room to yourselves."

They exchanged a glance. They didn't in the least mind the heat, they said. Elisabeth opened the door which faced south, and watched them walk away. Soon they vanished from view. She went upstairs, looked into the room which had already been got ready, the night before, and made sure that everything was as it should be. Then, through the half-closed shutters, she looked down into the garden. The silence was no different than it was always at this time of day. No human voice was audible. Not a twig snapped. There was nothing to be heard but the prevailing murmur of the fields, and one strenuous cicada, with, now and again, the song of a bird, broken off suddenly, as though it were singing in its sleep. Nothing betrayed their presence in the sleeping garden.

'They aren't making a sound: they certainly are not in the way.'

In this thought did Elisabeth find reassurance. All the same, she remembered how, as a young mother, she had always been nervous when Pierre played in silence. Had they nothing to say to one another? Where were they sitting? – on which of the benches? – or were they, perhaps, lying side by side in the grass?

Monsieur Gornac called up to her from the ground-floor. She gave a start, and pulled the shutters to, then closed the window.

"Here I am, father!"

He was in the billiard-room wearing his russet-coloured panama.

"I meant to go out, but this cursed heat made me come over a bit dizzy. I wanted to have a look from the terrace, just to see whether there's any sign of smoke over the heath. Go for me, will you, my dear? You know in which direction Le Bos lies? Better stand between the third and fourth lime. Splendid weather for the vines, but dam' awful for the trees!"

Every summer, for as far back as she could remember, he had suffered from this same tormenting uneasiness. If the sun blazed, then there was a threat of fire among the pines: if the weather was rainy, then the grapes would suffer. He might have run into Mademoiselle de la Sesque, she thought, and was on the point of trotting out the story of the breakdown which she had all ready for a long time. But the thought of the inevitable scene made her cowardly. After all, since the girl would not be dining at the house, and would not be in until long after Monsieur Gornac was asleep, it was better to take a chance and say nothing to him. He might not notice the presence of a stranger among them. He was unsociable, and hated strange faces, "skedaddled", as he put it, when a visitor was announced. If a car drove through the gate, he made his escape into the vines, and hid there until the enemy had cleared off.

"You'll come back and tell me, won't you, if you see smoke?"

Elisabeth crossed the courtyard, and was soon in the alley, under the trees. The young couple must be somewhere here, gone to ground within the small area between the trees, a clump on the right, the orchard on the left. Beyond, there was nothing but the vines under the washed-out blue of the sky. So heavy a torpor lay upon this little world that she would, she thought, have been able to hear the sound of their mingled breathing, the beating of their two hearts. She made her way along the lime-shaded path which prolonged the terrace to the East. She stopped between the third and fourth tree, facing that segment of the horizon where the family forests lay. She

raised her head, and gave a start. A murky veil hid the sky.
City folk would have taken it for a storm, but it did not take
her long to recognize, for what it was, the narrow column,
flecked with red, rising from the ground and spreading fanwise
over the dirty blue. At this moment a gust of wind from the
South rustled the withered leaves on the limes and brought a
smell of burning to the vineyard. She comforted herself with
the thought, which always, in these circumstances, calmed her
uneasiness.

'The fire's over Le Bos way: but it may well be thirty miles
beyond.'

It was impossible to calculate the distance to within ten miles
or so. The year when there had been forest fires at the sea's
edge, the wind had brought showers of ash as far as Viridis.

Still, she must go and report to her father-in-law.

'What a state he'll be in!'

She was thinking less of the pines, by this time possibly con-
sumed, than of old Gornac's unendurable agitation. She had
always been struck by the supernatural stillness brooding over
the vines on these torrid August afternoons, while, a few
miles away, the living forests were dying in a vast crackling of
burning wood. But to-day, she was more than ever aware of
the silence. Another fire, a very different fire, was smouldering
close at hand, a few feet away, perhaps, behind the nearby
privet. The forest blaze might, perhaps, spread towards Le Bos,
but it was not of those thousands of trees that she was thinking
now, but of two bodies, lying she knew not where – probably
within a stone's throw – so near the path on which she was
standing that, but for the South wind with its smell of burning
resin, she might have heard . . . what might she have heard?

She could not free her thoughts from that, though before
her eyes, as she stood there, was that vast spread of smoke

hanging over the heathland to which her heart was linked so firmly. She passed her hands over her damp face, looked at her arms, felt suddenly the weight of her thickening body. As she might have taken a fierce hold of herself had she felt herself on the point of fainting, she thought:

'If the Le Bos pines burn, we shall have to sell them at rock-bottom prices: with the seedlings, it'll be even worse – a dead loss. . . .'

But even this realization failed to shake her from her state of dazed bewilderment, from the mood of monstrous indifference which held her, motionless, in the middle of the path, under the mid-afternoon sun. She no longer recognized as something familiar the garden's stillness.

'I must go and break the news to father . . . he'll be beside himself. . . . How can a man so near to death, so close to the moment when he will have to say good-bye to all possessions, remain so completely occupied with the goods of this world?'

This Christian reflection had become a commonplace with her, but she never indulged in it except with reference to old Gornac, never applied it to herself. To-day, for the first time, she understood what "leaving everything behind" really meant. It came to her now that what was burning over there, in the distance, must, sooner or later, no matter what might happen, be torn from her; that, in very truth, she possessed nothing, was already stripped and naked, on this patch of unfeeling earth which, as she knew, her father-in-law had had carried, barrow-load by barrow-load, to cover the grave where, one day, they two would lie together, side by side, with Prudent, with Prudent's brother, with the two little coffins of her last-born. . . . What matter! Would not the young man and girl, hidden so close to her, be also, they two, separated at long last?

"No, that's not the same thing! . . . that's not the same

thing!..." she said aloud, in a low voice. She could not have explained what it was that she was feeling: it was vague even to herself. All love was ephemeral, but it seemed to her, in this mood that, in its essence, it meant an escape from the tyranny of time. Sooner or later, of course, we all have to go back into the general gaol of humankind, but the lover could at least say:

"For one moment I did break free: for one moment, if only one, I did live indifferent to life and death alike, to wealth and poverty, to good and evil, to glory and the shadow of the grave – hanging upon a breath. For that moment, one human face, appearing and disappearing, was all there was of night and day in my existence: for a brief while that, alone, was for me the measure of time: the regular thudding of my blood when I laid my head upon a shoulder, with my ear pressed to a pulsing artery."

She said again – "no, it's not the same thing" – though she could not explain how it was that death, which must tear her for ever from her vines and forests, had no such power over love – the love which she had never known. No matter what lay ahead of them, young Lagave and this girl of his would have had this timeless afternoon. How deep the silence was! The fancy came to her that it was not the August sun, but the young couple, who were holding time in abeyance and laying a sluggish torpor on the earth. Though all these thoughts were confused within her mind she was filled with a feeling of complete indifference for everything that, till to-day, had been her sole reality. So complete was her sense of detachment that it frightened her.

'I must be ill ... most certainly I must be ill ... or else, maybe, it is my change of life.'

She remembered one of her friends, a woman of sound

sense, who, round about her forty-eighth year, had been
generally thought to be out of her mind. She rubbed her bare
arm with her left hand, felt the curve of her buttocks, ran her
finger down her thigh.

'Enough of this silliness,' she said to herself: 'I must go and
break the news to father.'

But, looking once more towards Le Bos, she saw that the
column of smoke was showing thin against the blue. Only the
faintest hint of mist lay now above the heath. The fire had been
got under. There could be no point in worrying the old man.
Already, the world was waking. The round, red backs of
oxen could be seen coming from among the vines, and a man's
voice was calling them by their names.

'Enough of this silliness,' she thought again: 'enough of this
silliness.'

She went into the billiard-room.

"Cheer up, father: the sky is clearing over Le Bos."

Monsieur Gornac lifted his old head from the account-books
on the table before him. He said that when resin was dear one
needn't worry: the farmers kept their eyes skinned. Besides,
there were fewer and fewer herds now out on the heath.

"I've always held that it's the herdsmen as starts the fires."

She went out again. The sun, already low, lengthened her
shadow. She turned into the path to the right of the hornbeam
walk. Suddenly she saw them at the far end, the two young
people, making their way back to the house. They were silent,
but they walked like country lovers, with fingers inter-twined.
Paula was wearing a linen frock which clearly revealed her
long thighs with each step she took: her bare feet were pro-
tected by rope-soled shoes: there was blood on one of her
brown arms. The boy's shirt was open. A stab of pain brought

Elisabeth to a standstill. Her face could have betrayed nothing, however, for they smiled at her. They drew closer to one another. To her they seemed transparent, diaphanous. She had never seen eyes that looked so heavy, nor so turbid a moisture under human lids – so secret a look of ardour, weariness and guile. She had never seen any face at such close quarters, for never, until to-day, had she paid attention to living eyes. The stab came again : it made her raise her hand to her forehead. Bob cried to her:

"Qué calou!" (What heat!)

Paula ran her lips along her arm and said:

"My arm tastes salt."

Bob replied: – "I know that! . . . ." and both of them burst out laughing. Elisabeth told them not to come in yet. It would be just as well that Monsieur Gornac should not see them.

"I will bring you something to drink onto the terrace."

They thanked her casually. They were looking at one another, and no longer paying any attention to her. They went back down the slope, not bothering whether Elisabeth could see them or not. Soon they stopped, and, quite motionless, stood as though petrified, their two faces seemingly melted into one. And she, too, the heavy-bodied woman, half turned towards them, made no movement, but remained where she was, like a pillar of salt.

At last she went back to the house, entering it through the kitchen, so as to avoid old Gornac. The servants were sunk in siesta. In the pantry she filled a jug with cold water, picked up a bottle of orangeade and two glasses, and hurried back to the terrace. Paula de la Sesque showed solitary against the sky.

"Bob'll be back in a moment: he's just gone home to fetch his bathing things. We're going to drive down to the river.

He's going to have a swim, and then we'll go into Langon for dinner. He'll bring me back later. . . . What sort of time ought I to be in by? Have I permission to stay out till midnight?"

There was no hint of embarrassment in her voice. Obviously it had not occurred to her that there might be anything reprehensible in her behaviour. Elisabeth reassured her: when the weather was as hot as this she always went to bed late, so as to get the benefit of the cool night. As a matter of fact, it would be a good thing if the girl did not return until Monsieur Gornac was in bed and asleep.

"The door won't be locked. You needn't be afraid of the dog: he is always chained up."

Paula de la Sesque could see below the terrace, between the vines, the road along which Bob would come. She made a great effort to put on what Bob called one of her "high-hat acts".

"I shall never forget, madame, that we became engaged under your elms. . . ."

"Engaged! . . . but what about your parents?"

"It's not going to be easy . . . especially since I've had a proposal from the son of . . . but I'd better not mention any names . . . of one of the biggest landowners round Bazas. I expect you know him. Yes, it's going to be a great blow to them. . . . But, after all, they've never, in all their lives, thought about anything but their own pleasure!"

"My dear child . . . in a matter of this kind they will think only of you, of your happiness."

"I am the only judge of my happiness. You know Bob. . . ."

"He is a very nice boy . . . but, at your age, I should never have agreed to marry anyone so young. What I wanted was a steady man, a man who had been formed and made by life, somebody on whom I could lean. . . ."

These were the phrases which she had always heard used in her family. She uttered them now from force of habit. All the girls had, on principle, expressed contempt for a young husband, had aspired to nothing better than life with a "gentleman", with somebody secure in the possession of a solid position, important, corpulent and bald. She said again, "a man formed and made." Her eyes, like those of the girl, were fixed on the road. Paula broke in on her:

"*I* prefer a man I can *make* . . . and there'll be a lot of making to be done where Bob's concerned. Oh! I've no illusions: I love him as he is. . . . Here he comes!"

He was running, waving at the end of his naked arm a minute pair of bathing-shorts. Breathlessly he cried:

"Have you asked Madame Gornac?" . . .

"Really, Bob: *please*. . . ."

Paula was blushing. In reply to Elisabeth's question – "asked me what?" the young man, ignoring the girl's protests, explained that she was *frightfully* disappointed at not being able to bathe. She hadn't brought a bathing-dress – he said, and he had suggested that she ask Madame Gornac whether she might make use of Pierre's:

". . . a most respectable confection which covers him to the neck, she tells me: . . . saw it last year . . . a bit on the large side for Pierre, but you'll fill it out all right, Paula. . . ."

"You mustn't believe a word he says, madame: I was only joking."

She gave Bob a nudge with her elbow to stop him from going on.

And, indeed, not too soon, for a severe expression had appeared on Elisabeth's face. She turned away from them. She was shocked: at least, she thought she was shocked. Actually, the reason for her changed look was the picture, conjured up by these words, of her son, Pierre, small and skinny, in a bathing-suit too large for him and buttoned up to the chin. Paula, rather tactlessly, began to speak of him.

"When you next see your son, will you remember me to him? I did so enjoy the talk I had with him last year at a picnic! One doesn't often find a young man of that calibre at fashionable parties. . . . How stupid of you, Bob, to laugh like that. . . . What are you laughing *at*? You haven't been drinking, have you?"

"Yes, orangeade. I'm laughing for no particular reason. I suppose I'm free, aren't I, to laugh for no particular reason. After all, *you're* laughing!"

"What an idiot you are!"

They were laughing at her son, and Elisabeth felt hurt.

'They can't hold a candle to him' – she told herself.

They were not holding a candle to him, but chasing one another in the late afternoon light, there, on the blazing terrace, with the great spread of the heathland and the Sauterne country below them. She said:

"Better not get into a sweat if you're going to bathe. . . ."

Then she returned to the house without once looking back.

VI

"AREN'T you going upstairs, yet, my dear?"
"Not quite yet, father: I want to enjoy the cool of the evening."

"Beware of the dew: it's when one has been very hot during the day that one's most likely to catch cold. . . . Sure you hadn't better come up?"

It displeased Monsieur Gornac that his own habits should not have the force of law for everybody in the house. Elisabeth almost always gave in to his wishes. But to-night she had got to wait until the girl came back.

"Be careful to bolt the door, won't you?"

"Yes, father: don't fuss."

"If you get a chill, don't say I didn't warn you. I sometimes wonder how so active a woman as you can find pleasure in sitting in the dark, doing nothing. . . . But, after all, you're not a child. Good night."

He closed the hall-door behind him. She heaved a sigh. She was sitting on the bench just outside the house. A quiver of heat-haze reached as far as the road. Beyond, lay the shadowy mass of the hills, pricked here and there with lights. Laughter, cries, the sound of barking dogs rose from the still warm earth freed at last from the tyranny of the sun. Elisabeth's thoughts were vague; thoughts of a kind to which, until to-day, she had been a stranger. She was thinking that this evening, so seemingly like other evenings, would stay in the memory of the two young lovers until their dying day. Because of them, she could not help reading a solemn meaning into these evening hours. Since their laughter had died away, her mind had been full of them. They had set off in the car. By this time they must have reached Saint-Macaire and driven down to the river by the little lane which ran between two walls. Bob, no doubt, would have undressed behind a screen of willows, while she waited for him, seated on a stretch of gravel by the river bank. Again, that stab of pain. . . . 'Where are they now?' A solemn voice bade her good evening. By his stature she recognized the drover's eldest son. He went on his way down the slope towards the road, and she lost sight of him. For a while, however, she could hear his voice, and the sound of muffled laughter in reply. Someone was waiting for him in the meadows. She looked up at the swarming heavens, at the black stretch, as of a curtain, nibbled into holes as far as eye could see, devoured by a multitude of pallid worlds. She did not know of what, nor why, she felt frightened. Now, at forty-eight her eyes had been opened. For the first time, she had learned the meaning of loneliness. She had suddenly woken up like a sleep-walker to find herself upon the edge of a roof, on the brink of an abyss, with no rail other than a beloved body to protect her against people and darkness and the great unknown. How easy must it be for two beings united in the flesh to be brave! The voices fell silent, the laughter died away. . . . One by one, the lights went out until the hills were no more than a denser darkness in the dark. A late moon rose over the slumbering lanes. One solitary cock sounded a warning to all his fellows in the country of Benauge. She was conscious of the cold, and went into the house, but did not shoot the bolt, because of Paula. In the drawing-room the lamp was lit. She felt reassured and sat down in her usual chair, opened the basket full of linen waiting to be darned, and felt for her spectacles.

The room was large, and the light left the corners in darkness. The rosewood chairs stood in a circle round a small mahogany table. Moths, blinded by the lamp, were beating against the shade. She had a horror of moths, but could not close the windows. The night air must be free to enter. It was more precious than water in the desert, and would stay here in the room until the next evening.

"At nine in the morning," Elisabeth always said; "I shut up the whole house."

Terror of darkness came with the moths into the gloomy interior. Elisabeth laid down her work, and murmured:

"What can that child be up to?"

Ten o'clock had sounded some while back. "Alone under the night sky with that boy. . . . Ah! I ought never to have . . ."

Thus did she call on the proprieties: but what really drew her to the door was the longing not to be alone. She stared into the darkness and let herself believe that the rustle of leaves was the sound of footsteps. But no one was there. Where were they? What were they doing? Again, that visitation of intolerable pain.

'Betrothal . . . *my* betrothal.'

She looked at the drawing-room, whither, once or twice, she had come from Beautiran to spend a couple of hours with her intended. On each occasion her parents had come in the evening to fetch her, for it is not decent for two engaged young people to sleep under the same roof. Just an hour with Prudent on the sofa! The door had always been left open, and in the room next door, Madame Lavignasse had sat listening. Sometimes she had coughed and called out:

"I don't hear a sound!"

But they were not kissing. The simple truth was that they had nothing to say to one another. Elisabeth raised her shoulders in a shrug. A fit of laughter shook her. Ever since earliest girlhood she had been well guarded. A young girl must never be left alone. Her governess had always been on duty outside the lavatory door to see that she did not stay in it too long. Never alone! Yet, Mademoiselle de la Sesque had the reputation of being more serious minded than her companions!

'She'll come in when it suits her. When she does, I shall give her a piece of my mind, but not until after I have told her never to show herself here again. She is leaving to-morrow, and good riddance to her!'

This time she was not deceived: somebody was walking up the path. The dog barked. Elisabeth hurriedly laid down her work and went into the hall.

"Here you are at last, my child: I was beginning to get anxious."

But the voice that answered her was a man's:

"Why do you say 'vous' to me, mamma?"

"Is that you, Pierre?"

"Who else should it be?"

"But why are you turning up so late? The last train got in almost an hour ago."

Pierre Gornac had followed her into the drawing-room.

"I've been boxed up all day in this frightful heat. I felt I should like a bit of a walk in the moonlight. I left my luggage at the station, and came up on foot through the vines."

"Why do you never let me know when you are coming? It would make everything so much easier. But you don't like putting yourself out."

"Must you start criticizing me so soon?"

"I'm not criticizing you, dear. It's for your own sake that I said what I did. I would have had something for you to eat. . . . Oh, you've had dinner, have you? . . . well, in that case hadn't you better go straight to bed? You must be worn out."

She was impatient for him to be safely shut away in his

room. The la Sesque girl might turn up at any moment. . . .
Ought she to tell him about the breakdown: Pierre was standing close to the lamp, a thin figure with patches of sweat on his
bony face. Each time she saw her son after an absence, he always
looked uglier than she remembered.

"Do, at least, go and have a wash."

His answer sounded dry:

"I will: then, perhaps, you'll give me a kiss."

She quickly went to him and stood on tip-toe:

"What a silly you are, my poor darling. . . . Heavens! how
you've grown. . . . I really think you're taller than last time
you were here!"

"Four foot six: not an inch more in five years. Why must
you always say that when I come home? I shan't grow any
taller!"

"Sit down: would you like something to drink?"

"No."

"Or to eat?"

"I've told you already that I have had dinner."

"Did you have a comfortable journey? No coughing? no
nose-bleeding?"

Pierre was walking up and down, shaking his head irritably.
'Mamma thinks only of my health,' he was thinking: 'that's
the only thing that matters to her.'

Then, suddenly:

"You haven't asked me whether my meetings were a success. . . ."

"How sensitive you are! Well, were they?"

He pretended not to notice the irony in her voice, and
answered:

"Yes, they were, very. At Limoges I had a set to with a
Communist, and carried the whole audience with me. The

Communist shook me by the hand. . . . I had more trouble
with the Royalists, at Angers. . . ."

"Oh, do sit down instead of walking round in circles! . . .
you make me feel quite dizzy. . . . What would you say to a
glass of orangeade?"

"If you insist. . . ."

He sat down, his long body leaning forward, his elbows on
his knees, his fingers in his mouse-coloured hair which needed
cutting. His mother had already gone to the door, but he called
her back.

"By the bye, mamma, is it true that the Lagave boy is staying
with his grandmother?"

She stood stock-still, with one hand on the latch:

"Why do you ask?"

"Because if it was him I started like a hare under the terrace,
with a girl in tow, I'll have something to say to the young
blackguard in the morning. He'd jolly well better keep his
beastliness to his grandmother's house."

It had not occurred to him that his mother might not share
his indignation. All the same, he was more angry than aston-
ished when she answered:

"You're always imputing evil . . . evil is your first thought,
always. Judge not that ye be not judged."

"But look here, mamma: the fellow's a rotter: you know
that as well as I do . . . or, no: perhaps, on second thoughts,
you don't know what I know."

"What do you know?"

"In Paris, thank God, I live in a very different circle from
that of our charming gentleman. All the same, I can't help
hearing a certain amount of scandal. This neighbour of ours,
let me tell you, is notorious. On one occasion I heard a friend
of mine, speaking of somebody else, say – 'by and large, he's

one of the Bob Lagave type.' Poor mamma, nobody as saintly as you could possibly understand what *that* means!"

Elisabeth was quite taken aback by the violence of her irritation. It rose from the depth of her being as she listened to this sniggering, self-important son of hers, who stood there making the joints of his fingers crack. He had Prudent Gornac's habit of shuffling when he walked.

"How d'you know that the boy hasn't been misrepresented? I haven't noticed anything particularly bad about him. Anyone as good-looking as he is has probably broken any number of hearts, and I imagine that among the people he frequents in Paris, women scorned don't stop at much when they want to get their own back!"

"It really is quite incredible! . . ."

"What's incredible? Oh, Pierre, for Heaven's sake don't crack your fingers like that: it makes me want to scream!"

"To think I should have to come all the way to Viridis to hear my mother deliver a panegyric of this . . . of this . . ."

He spluttered and stuttered, unable to find the right word with which to express his disgust, his contempt. He moved about the room with bent back, bumping into the chairs, raising his voice, and, unconsciously, in tone and gesture, becoming the public orator engaged in controversy. The very excess of Elisabeth's enraged reaction suddenly reminded her of the resolution she had made, of the decision she had taken, not to oppose Pierre. Unfortunately, before she had had time to take a hold on herself, he, with his very first words, had released in her the accumulated charge of hostility. She now grasped his hands.

"Pierre, my dear, what *is* the sense in our going on like this? You know perfectly well that we share the same ideas, you and I, the same faith. . . ."

But he broke free:

"No! you are like every other woman: yes, you, Madame Prudent Gornac, President of the Christian Mothers' Union. When it comes to debauchery, you are all indulgence. . . . You find something charming in the idea of a young man on the loose. . . ."

"Pierre! . . . *please!*"

"And, to make matters worse, you believe that you are religious! You lay claim to a knowledge of what sin means. . . . Why, you don't know the first thing about it! . . . It seems never to have occurred to you that a young man whose only concern in this world is to seduce others, to soil others, to lead them to damnation, is a murderer – worse, even, than a murderer!"

He uttered a mocking laugh, flung out his arms with fists clenched, and gave the impression that he was stamping up and down a platform. No doubt, in imagination, he could see between the elm-trees and the vines, fleeing before him in the moonlight, a youth intent on ravishing a willing victim. And it was upon his own land, in the grass where he would lie to-morrow, that two guilty bodies would collapse in the very ecstasy of desire, indifferent to the sky above them, to the stars which bore witness to an infinity of power and glory.

"Listen to me, my son . . . you are right. But I beg you to be calm: you terrify me. . . ."

"Why not say straight out that I am a fanatic, a ranter? Advise me, as you always do, to dose myself with valerian, or to take a tablet of aspirin in a hot infusion of lime-tea, and to try to get some sleep. I know you so well! the only thing in me you are concerned about, is my body. You think only of my physical health. Even your religion is part and parcel of your comfort, of your rules of hygiene. . . ."

Elisabeth had chosen the way of gentleness, and nothing now would make her depart from it.

"Pierre, look at me. . . . I want you to look at me."

She took his face between her hands. Suddenly, tears began to run down the hollow, yellow cheeks, unshaven since the previous evening, blackened by a growth of stubble, stained with sweat and coal-dust – tears, which were like those of a child. Thanks to his extreme purity, Pierre was very close to childhood, its climate hung about him still. For a moment, he looked his age – scarcely more than twenty-two.

His mother forced him to lay his head upon her shoulder:

"What is my boy so unhappy about?" she said.

At that, he gave up the struggle. He recognized as something long known and familiar, the smell that came from his mother, the smell of a knitted shawl which once his childhood's tears had moistened. But he noticed that her stroking of his hair was absent-minded, that her thoughts were wandering – occupied with what he did not know. Not once, since he had come into this room, had Elisabeth ceased to listen for footsteps in the darkness. She had thought she heard the creak of gravel, then, a return of silence. She imagined that Paula and Bob, taken unaware by Pierre's return, were waiting outside, with ears pricked, waiting for him to go to his room, before entering the hall. But there was nothing to show that he was intending to do any such thing. He wiped his face with a dirty handkerchief, and started once more to walk up and down, snuffling. Elisabeth followed him with her eyes. When would he make up his mind to go to bed? But she kept herself from saying anything, relied now only on her silence to discourage him, to prompt him to seek rest in sleep. At length, unable to stand any more, she pretended to stifle a yawn, looked at her watch, aped surprise:

"Close on eleven! The candles are on the billiard-table: won't you go up?"

"Not yet: I'll stay down here for a bit. My nerves are all on edge. I shouldn't sleep. . . ."

There was nothing now that Elisabeth could do but embark on the story of the breakdown. Why hadn't she begun with it? Pierre would not understand why she had waited so long before explaining matters. She spoke, stumbling over the words:

"Actually, I can't go up yet, either. My mind must have been wandering. We've had quite a little adventure here, and I entirely forgot to tell you about it! . . ."

Pierre was not listening. He stood with his face half turned to the door. He said:

"Odd: there's somebody walking in the garden . . . who can it be so late? . . . But there is somebody, I heard laughter. . . . It really would be the last straw . . ."

He was already half way across the hall when the front-door opened. Elisabeth, her heart pounding, could not utter a word. She heard Pierre call out:

"Who's there?"

Then, Paula's voice:

"Don't you recognize me? Hasn't Madame Gornac told you?"

The girl went into the drawing-room, followed by the young man. He shot a questioning look at his mother, who made a pretence of laughing:

"This is what comes of starting a quarrel before I'd even had time to tell you our Viridis news. I suppose you think nothing ever happens here: Why, we've had a car accident, here, on our very doorstep, my dear . . . a lucky accident, because it has given me an opportunity of getting to know this charming cousin of ours, whom you've been so eloquent about. . . ."

She was talking too much. There was something unnatural in her sprightliness. Pierre had never known her to be like this. She, too, realized that she was playing a part. Surely, she had never used just this voice since the Convent days when, on Reverend Mother's Feast, she had taken part in private Theatricals?

"What car accident?"

Pierre's gaze shifted to the young girl who was now standing silent in the shadows, so that he could not see her face. Then he looked again at his mother, all high colour and talkativeness. Mademoiselle de la Sesque had thrown a beige travelling coat with a pattern of large checks about her shoulders. The lamp clearly revealed the white cotton frock which was now crumpled and marked with grass-stains. Pierre could feel that her eyes were upon him. He was conscious of a sense of shame, of distress. He became acutely aware of his wrists, of his untidy hair, of the town suit which, all day long, had been so terribly hot. Whenever a woman stared at him he at once became conscious of himself, of everything about himself, of his clothes, of his body. He felt dreadfully uncomfortable. He wished he could disappear.

"I'll tell you exactly what happened. Mademoiselle de la Sesque's car . . ."

Pierre paid not the slightest attention to what his mother was saying. He had drawn closer to the girl. He was looking at the white frock with its stains of crushed grass. . . . It was a white dress that he had seen a while back, running in the moonlight between the hornbeams and the vines. So that was it! . . . He found courage now to raise his eyes. He laughed mockingly, like a young man who has not been taken in. She must have noticed this, for she cut Elisabeth short:

"Forgive me, madame, but you are a bad liar ... you are not used to lying! Don't you think that your son is old enough to understand – and excuse? ... Well, to cut a long story short, there was somebody at Viridis whom I just had to see, and your mother was kind enough to give us the run of her garden. ... Oh!" – she added with a comic look of fear – "please don't look like that! I give you my word that the meeting was the most innocent thing in the world. ..."

Pierre interrupted her with his nervous, jerky laugh:

"Permit me to express a doubt: innocent? an innocent meeting with somebody like our honourable neighbour? ... I beg your pardon, but to speak of innocence in such a connexion."

"Please say no more."

She took a tortoise-shell case from the pocket of her coat, helped herself to a cigarette, and lit it at the lamp which momentarily revealed the sunburned face which youth and a tell-tale weariness made charming. She went on, in an affected voice:

"I really must stop you before you make a fool of yourself: we're engaged."

"You? – engaged to young Lagave? – you?"

From the darkest corner in the room, where the sofa stood, Madame Gornac's voice broke in:

"Do you think that if they hadn't been engaged I should have allowed ...?"

But Pierre, without hearing her, went on:

"You, engaged to Bob Lagave? That's a good joke, that is! You must be laughing at me!"

"You're all the same, you enthusiastic democrats!" – the girl exclaimed: "last year, at that pic-nic, you talked an awful lot about Working Men's Colleges, and the breaking down of

the class barrier – and a whole lot of stuff of the same kind, and
now, here you are, the first to object because a young woman
has had the idea of marrying somebody who is not her social
equal . . . you're just a humbug!"

Her cigarette had made her cough. She laughed, and looked
Pierre up and down with a mocking expression which made
him furious.

"You're deliberately pretending not to understand me. It is
not because his grandmother is an old peasant woman that
Robert Lagave seems to me to be unworthy of you. I'd far
rather see you married to the butcher's boy at Viridis – far
rather!"

"What's the matter with you, Pierre? – are you mad?"

Elisabeth had emerged from her dark corner and seized his
arm: but he threw her off.

"No, I am not mad. I say again that any man of the People
would make her a better husband than . . ."

"What harm has Bob Lagave ever done you? I am perfectly
aware that he's no innocent . . . he's had his adventures . . .
what of it? . . . there's nothing so awful about that. Let's go one
worse, and say he's thoroughly debauched. That, I can assure
you, doesn't begin to shock me."

"That I can well believe: you're all the same!"

Pierre, by this time, had lost control of himself, and was
gesticulating wildly. His mother told him to keep his voice
lower if he didn't want to wake his grandfather, and he quiet-
ened down. But this seemed only to make him angrier than
ever.

"As I was saying to my mother a short while ago, you
women think a great deal more of profligates than of those who
are self-respecting, who have ideals, faith. Judging by what
you have said, debauchery is the only thing young men are

interested in. You know nothing of the splendid young fellows who are alive with enthusiasm for great causes, who are capable of delicacy, loyalty, who observe a scrupulous standard of behaviour. They respect women and worship them, instead of spattering them with filth. . . ."

"What a truly remarkable orator you are, monsieur!"

He broke off short, and passed a hand over his forehead.

"You think me a figure of fun, don't you?"

"Oh, dear me, no! There's a deal of truth in what you say. Yes" – she went on, with a thoughtful air: "it may even be that quite decent women don't set much store by virtue in a man: they may pretend to, just to show them how grateful they are to them for showing their respect. But, fundamentally, what we all of us want is to be desired, stared at, pursued. We are born into this world as game for the hunter: by nature, we are the prey of the strong. . . . Don't turn away like that: sit down, and let us talk together as friends – won't you?"

Pierre obeyed. But even when seated he could not keep still. The movement of his legs made the table shake: he rubbed his hands together till his finger-joints cracked. As though to tame him, Paula offered her cigarette-case: but he refused it.

"What! not even tobacco? You must be in training for canonization . . . no, no, I was only joking. . . . Take that look of fury off your face, and listen to me. I have no illusions about Bob, monsieur: I know him. He frequents a rotten set: he is a poor, helpless child, the victim of a pretty face and an appealing eye. . . . I spoke about game for the hunter . . . that's exactly what *he* is, poor kid! I know that well enough. He loves me because I am a refuge for him, because I can give him peace of mind. He has often told me so, just as, often, he wants me to talk to him about the years ahead, when he will no longer be quite so charming, nor quite so young. In me he will find the same calm, quiet love. . . . Why are you laughing?"

Once again Pierre Gornac was on his feet, choking with indignation:

"I tell you again that you do *not* know him . . . there are degrees in debauchery. You don't begin to know him . . . you *can't* – because, no matter how free a life you may lead, you can be only what you are – a young girl!"

He repeated the words – "a young girl", on a note of adoration. But either Paula did not notice it, or felt no gratitude for this tribute. She, too, was standing, with both her hands on the table, leaning forward. Her face, with the light beating full on it, looked so deeply stricken, that Pierre fell silent, suddenly sobered.

"This time," she said, "you've got to say what you mean. Come on, out with it!"

He no longer dared to look her in the face. He moved away from the lamp to the window.

"You have been warned: it's none of my business now."

He made as though to lean out into the darkness.

"How good the night smells!" – he said.

But Paula would not let him alone:

"You have either said too much, or not enough! I insist on your saying straight out what is in your mind!"

He shook his head. Elisabeth did her best to come to the rescue.

"Midnight! off to bed, children! By to-morrow morning we shall have forgotten all about this. . . ."

"No, madame: I cannot go on living under the shadow of these insinuations. Come along, monsieur, out with it! – I am listening."

"And I, Pierre, order you not to say another word!"

"I swear to you, madame, that I shall not leave this room until he has spoken aloud all that he is thinking! This time, I want to know: and I'm going to know!"

It was true. For a long time now she had wanted to know. Bob was not the only young man with an ugly reputation: but she had more than once intercepted smiles at his expense, had been made aware that all that might be said was not being said. It was as though among all the rackety young men of his age he occupied a place apart. These indications, taken by themselves, would not have deeply worried her. Nothing which had not reached her from Bob's own lips, could strike roots in her, so certain was she that the infant whom she loved had nothing in common with the young man who played about in bars and dance-halls with American women. But she had a vivid memory of the very day, of the very hour when, for the first time she had felt genuinely uneasy. It had been early in the previous Spring, at Versailles. He had been driving the car at a slow pace along the Great Canal. Her eyes had been fixed on his bare hands gripping the wheel, powerful hands, gentle hands. She had taken one of them in her own, holding it as though it were the token of her happiness. Suddenly a wave of tenderness had come over her. So strong had her feeling been that she could not resist a sudden desire to touch it with her lips. But as though the feel of them had burned him, Bob had snatched his hand away so violently that the car had swerved. His voice, when he spoke, had been harsh.

"No! no! you must be mad!"

She could not understand why so simple a gesture should have been distasteful to him, nor why he had said:

"The idea of your kissing my hand, Paula! ... I'm not worthy...."

This humility in him at first had touched her – it made her feel happy to know that he did more than want her, that he worshipped her. And, so it was that, when they had left the car, and had walked together as far as the Grand-Trianon, with Bob still taciturn, she had suddenly, by a surprise stroke, taken possession of both his hands:

"This time I've got the two of them, whether you like it or not!"

But again he had broken free, and on his face there was a look of suffering.

"Darling, I do beg of you . . . you don't know how awful you make me feel. . . ."

The girl had protested, but he had cut her short. What he had then said had often, since that day, come back into her memory.

"You don't know me, Paula: you don't know what I am!"

Later, whenever she had tried to kiss his hand, her gesture had provoked the same withdrawal, the same uprush of humility and shame. She had often thought about all this when she was alone. And so, this evening, she had made up her mind not to let the wretched Pierre Gornac get away until he had voided all his venom. What he had to say, she felt sure, would amount to no more than the retailing of scraps of dirty gossip. How should her darling not be hated by those who never had been, and never would be, loved? Yes, scraps of filthy gossip: but whatever that gossip was, she wanted to get to the bottom of it. It was child's play for her to make Pierre fly off the handle. She said to him now that it was easy enough to make insinuations, but that she was quite determined to rub his nose in his own lies.

"Lies? lies? – all right, then; listen. But I give you fair warning that it's going to hurt: that you will bear me resentment for what I am going to say."

She shook her head, and he added with deep earnestness:
"Remember, it's you who have insisted."

Again she protested that she *ordered* him to speak. How often,
later, when the irreparable had happened, was Pierre to recol-
lect that moment, if only to gain reassurance, to free his conscience from a sense of guilt.

'I would so much rather have said nothing: but she would
not have it so.'

VII

"I CANNOT say what I have to say in front of you, mamma. Shall we go out on the terrace, mademoiselle? It is a warm night."

"Cover up well, my boy" – said Madame Gornac.

Then she helped Paula into her coat, and, since Pierre was already in the hall, suddenly drew the girl to her.

"I wish you'd stay here ... what can it matter to you what people are saying? I have known this Bob of yours ever since he was a child ... he is a good boy, a poor, unfortunate boy...."

Paula repeated the words:

"A poor, unfortunate boy...."

She hesitated. Standing there in the drawing-room where, so recently, their angry voices had been loudly raised, she could hear only the murmur of the sleeping countryside. A dog barked. She looked across the road to where, between the trees, Madame Lagave's house shone white in the radiance of a waning moon. She could see, in imagination, Bob's room, though she had never entered it: the bed-recess which he had so often described to her, the ship's cot in which he had slept as a schoolboy on holiday, the flimsy pyjamas which were such a cause of irritation to his grandmother. She knew that he lay there with his hands crossed upon his breast. She could see those hands and, on the right one, a ring she had given him, a dark cameo with the colour of dried blood: the long fingers of a smoker, rather tawny hands, rather freckled hands, hands which she loved too much though he would not give her the right to kiss them.

It was then that Pierre, who had opened the front-door, called to her, then that she uttered in reply the one word which set the seal upon her destiny:

"Coming!"

Seated far from the lamp, upon the sofa, Elisabeth's whole attention was centred on the sound of their receding footsteps, which not for a single moment did she cease to hear. Sometimes a raised voice, an exclamation, reached her. How lucky that old Gornac was hard of hearing, and that his room faced North! What a loud voice her poor Pierre had! It was the only one of the two that was distinctly audible. She remembered the silence of the afternoon, when not so much as a sigh had disturbed the pair of young creatures so deeply drowned in love. People who were not in love had no scruple about breaking the stillness of the night, but would speak all at once, and then, suddenly, stop. But there were moments when the two adversaries must have paused for breath, and then she could hear only the empty land under the sky in the hour before dawn. Though she was not accustomed to sit up late, she felt no desire for sleep. It was impossible for her to keep her thoughts on anything but the noisy couple in the darkness. She was waiting for them to come back, and kept her mind from Pierre, as though she feared that she might hate him. Why was he meddling? Who had given him the right to interfere? What could he understand of love? Love was no concern of his: he scarcely knew what the word meant, being sprung from a race whose members are strangers to passion. But he was always ready to instruct others! – that was his form of pleasure, and even a man like him must have some pleasure in life. She felt herself becoming sarcastic. She laughed to herself. All the same, she was suffering, was reproaching herself for not having prevented Pierre from talking. It was for her to protect the boy who was sleeping on the other side of the road. There was no need for her, as there was for Paula, merely to imagine the room in which the outstretched body lay: she had been in it many times (in Bob's absence during the winter months, Maria Lagave liked to move into it because it looked South). She remembered having sat upon the bed, and thought about it now with an absent look in her eyes. Suddenly the lamp flickered; it had come to the end of its oil. A horrible stench filled the room. She turned down the wick till it expired, after first lighting the candles in the sconces. She shuddered in the funereal glow, and closed the window.

The footsteps were drawing nearer, but there was no sound of voices now. The crunching of the gravel filled the night. Perhaps it had woken the Galberts. Those between whom no love is lost think little about concealment. The man and the girl came into the room. In his usual voice he said:

"One can't see a thing in here! . . . is there no oil in the house?"

Elisabeth could see at once that Paula had been crying. The fatigues of a highly emotional day, the events of the evening, the exhaustion produced by an interminable postponement of bed-time – these things had left their marks on the girl's face. It had suddenly grown older, and looked almost ugly. Pierre was again talking, pretentiously and volubly. He was saying that in matters of this sort, one could never have absolute proof. No doubt, when public opinion was unanimous that might be held to supply adequate justification of belief: all the same, personal investigation would be far more satisfactory, though he did not see what form it could take. He hoped, he said, that his conclusions might be shown to be wrong. . . .

"For God's sake, Monsieur, don't follow me about like that! – and do stop talking for a *moment*: I feel quite deaf!"

These words brought him to a halt, though Paula continued
to wander about the dimly-lit room. She was holding the travel-
ling-coat wrapped round her with her two hands. Madame
Gornac went into the hall, and came back with a candle which
she gave to her son:

"You have done quite enough damage for one night. Now
go to bed . . . go!"

Pierre took the candle, but still did not make a move. He
was following with his eyes the shivering little creature who
kept stumbling against the furniture.

"I thought that I was acting for the best . . . I am quite sure
that I *did* act for the best. Some day you will be grateful to
me: my conduct was prompted solely by a sense of duty. . . ."

"Oh yes, I've no doubt you thought you were doing your
duty: you always do – and now you'd better go to bed."

"Besides, it was you, mademoiselle, who insisted. . . ."

Without so much as looking at him, Paula went across to
Elisabeth:

"*Please* tell him to go away . . . *please* tell him to go away!
. . ."

He left the room. They could hear the noise made by his
boots on the wooden stairs. A door on the first floor banged.
Elisabeth waited until silence had once more descended upon
the house. Then she moved to Paula's side, drew her down upon
the sofa, and, suddenly, felt against her the impact of a body
shaken by tears. She asked no questions, but stroked the girl's
shaven nape, being careful not to interrupt the flow of her
words:

"I know perfectly well how Bob earns his living: I have been
in some of the houses he's arranged: people pay a lot for that
sort of thing nowadays. It's easy enough to say it's just kindness
on their part. *Of course* much of the work comes to him from

rich friends . . . it's a blessing he *does* know a lot of extremely rich men and women . . . in a job like that one can only get commissions from people used to luxurious living. . . ."

She was talking, as she might have sung, to keep her courage up, alone at night in a wood. Suddenly:

"What your son has told me is horrible. He says everyone knows about it. He says . . ."

Once again she was shaken with sobs and could not go on. Elisabeth held her in a close embrace. She wiped her cheeks with her own handkerchief.

"My child, I'd rather not hear any more: I beg you not to repeat to me what that wretched Pierre told you. Look at me: whatever it may have been, it can be of no conceivable importance. Don't shake your head. I give you my word that what I say is true – of no importance whatever. These are matters about which I have never thought: consequently, I have only very vague ideas about them. You must give me time to think. . . . How can I make you understand? . . . Listen to me: the life of a boy like Bob, no matter what it's like, doesn't matter. You know him, don't you? you love him for what he is, don't you? – why, then, take one fault, one bad tendency, and isolate it in your mind? It makes me miserable to think that I cannot convince you of what I feel so profoundly. See, I am prepared to stand up for him as though he were my own son. . . . Maybe I am too indulgent . . . but I can't help thinking that there is nothing we should not be ready to accept in one who has made our heart his prisoner. If Bob were not a poor, defenceless child, you would not love him as you do. . . ."

"You see, madame, even you believe, admit, that there are things in his life. . . ."

"I believe nothing, I admit nothing. . . . What business is it of yours?"

Paula looked at her in amazement.

"What would your son say if he could hear you now? Can we feel contempt and love for the same person? Can one marry a man for whom one can have no real respect? . . ."

She asked the question. It was so purely conventional, so almost "official", that Elisabeth was taken aback.

"But, since you *do* love him!" – she protested, with a somewhat bewildered air: "when one admits that one loves, there is no more to be said: in love there is room for everything, or so it seems to me. Respect for the man one loves? . . . Forgive me if I say that to me such words are quite meaningless. I must think: when one loves . . ."

She repeated the words – "when one loves" – with a fleeting smile which flooded the heavy, flabby face with a light which nobody, till then, had ever seen in it. But Paula was beyond noticing what Elisabeth was saying, or how she was looking. Seated at the other end of the sofa, with her elbows on her knees, she seemed to be deep sunk in thought.

"I have quite made up my mind what to do," she said at last: "I shall leave as soon as it is light, without seeing Bob again. . . ."

"Without seeing him? . . ."

"Oh, the separation won't be for long . . . just long enough to let me ask a few questions and write a few letters. There are two or three points I must get clear. When they are out of the way, then I shall be able to look him in the face again."

"My child, surely you can't be going to cause him such terrible pain?"

"Do you think it won't be painful for me, too? But I *must* know the truth about the man I am going to marry!"

"But you know that already, since you love him. What do *actions* matter? Listen, I have just remembered something. . . ."

Once upon a time we had as curé here a young priest, a dis-
tinguished and highly educated man, but a man, above all, of
great goodness and delicacy of feeling. His sermons went
straight to the hearts of his listeners: there seemed to be no end
to his charity: he devoted his life to working among the young,
and they adored him. Then, one day, we were amazed to hear
that he had had to make a very hasty departure – some scandal
or other. . . . All the people of Viridis were loud in their con-
demnation (I not the least). 'What a hypocrite!' we said: 'how
carefully he covered up his real self! How convincing all that
charity of his was! How cleverly he took us all in!' Well, I
have often thought about him since then, and especially,
though I don't know why, in the course of the last few days.
As a result of my thinking I came to the conclusion that that
poor young priest had, in fact, not taken us in at all. He had
really been what we took him to be, good, compassionate,
selfless – but, with all that, he had *also* been capable of a sinful
act. . . ."

There was a dryness in Paula's voice, as she said:

"I don't see the connexion. . . ."

Elisabeth passed her hand over her forehead:

"You must forgive me: I don't really know why I told you
all that . . . perhaps I thought it might be of some help, should
you find something in the life of your fiancé. . . ."

"My fiancé? . . . Oh, not yet, madame!"

Elisabeth could think of nothing more to say. All of a sudden she felt the weight of her weariness, the urgency of her
desire for sleep, the burden of an exhaustion beyond anything
she could find words to express. She got up and fetched Paula
some letter-paper, then sank again onto the sofa, while the girl
set herself to write, standing at the mantelpiece, by the light
of the candles.

"You'll tell him, won't you, my dear, that you are coming back?"

"Of course, madame."

"And mention a definite date? Uncertainty will be the worst thing for him: he is still very weak."

Paula hesitated, nibbling her pen:

"Do you think that three weeks . . . ?"

"Three weeks! you must be mad! – a fortnight at the very most. . . ."

Elisabeth could feel in her heart and in her flesh something of the pain so soon to strike at the boy now sleeping on the other side of the road, with his head on his bent arm. For his sake she was suffering as his mother might have done. She grew excited at the thought of attempting even the impossible so that he should not lose his Paula. The feeling that she was wholly disinterested reassured her. The fact that she felt no jealousy gave her an obscure sense of happiness.

"Well, *that's* done: would you be so very kind as to see that this note reaches him? . . . Oh, forgive me, madame, I ought not to have stuck down the flap of the envelope: I wasn't thinking what I was doing. And now, I shall try to get a little rest. . . . It will be quite unnecessary to wake me: I am certain I shan't sleep a wink! Besides, the dawn can't be far off."

"You must have something to eat before you start. . . . You can't leave without having a hot drink. . . ."

Paula declared that there was no need to arrange breakfast for her, that she would stop at Langon. Madame Gornac took the candles, went ahead of the girl as far as her bedroom door, and kissed her on the forehead. When she reached her own room, the pious lady knelt down, as she did every night before going to sleep, and buried her face in the sheets.

Come, Holy Spirit, fill the hearts of Thy faithful servants, and kindle in them the fire of Thy divine love. Prostrate at Thy feet, O God, I render thanks unto Thee that Thou hast given me a heart to know Thee and love Thee inasmuch as Thou hast kept me and watched over me all my life long. . . . She had said that she loved him, and now she was going away without seeing him again. She knew that she was loved, that that happiness was hers, yet she was going away for no better reason than that the boy had been spoiled by others, had let himself be coddled and made much of. The little fool really thought she loved him. . . . *Forgive me, O Lord, for not thinking only of Thee. Let us search our hearts, and, after offering up our worship to God, ask of Him.* . . . Is there no way in which I could send word to him before Paula leaves? If she sees him, he will win her back. If only I could delay her departure until he has come to her! She will yield once she has seen him again. I must think. But first I must finish my prayer. *O God! I repent with all my heart the sins I have committed against Thy adorable Majesty, and very humbly I implore Thy pardon.* . . . She will start at the earliest possible moment. As soon as it is light, I must find some excuse for getting into Maria Lagave's house. But what excuse? I don't mind betting that the old she-goat is already imagining things. . . . *I know not whether death will come to me this night, but into Thy hands, O God, I commend my spirit. Judge me not according to Thine anger.* . . . What possible reason could there be for me to go knocking at Maria's door at five o'clock in the morning? . . . *Pardon me all my past sins. I hold them all in detestation. I promise that until the moment of my latest breath I will be faithful unto Thee, and that my wish is to live only for Thee, my Lord and my God.* . . . To be thinking such thoughts while saying my prayers, is disgraceful. I am being punished for having shown too great a sympathy. Once one starts meddling . . . It's their mess, after all, and they must get out of it. How far had I got? *Saints who rejoice before the throne of God in heaven* . . . no. I'll skip that part. . . . *Dear Guardian Angel whom God sent to watch over me and keep me* . . . besides, I've got no excuse to give Maria Lagave . . . still, if I wake up early enough . . .

Elisabeth Gornac always maintained that she could wake at the precise minute she had fixed upon when she had fallen asleep. If, this time, the miracle did not occur, the reason probably was that she had not sufficiently desired it. Before sleep came to her, she had found pleasure in the thought that, with Paula gone, Bob would feel lost and abandoned, that only in her company would he forget his pain. One of these days, she told herself, he would say: "Young girls don't know what love means . . ." That would be on the terrace, at ten o'clock in the morning. She could imagine his face, looking still pale, but no longer contorted by anguish. . . . "What a fool I am!" she said in a low voice, and rolled over heavily to face the wall.

VIII

THE daylight woke her, light so leaden that she thought it still was dawn. But her watch showed eight o'clock. This mist might equally well presage torrid heat or storms of rain. Someone was moving about in the courtyard. Not doubting for a moment that it was Bob, she hurriedly put on her dressing-gown, pinned up her hair, powdered her face which was puffy with sleep, ran to the window and pushed back the shutters. She had been right: Bob stood below, dressed in white flannels, looking up.

"At last! Where is Paula? Has she driven into Langon?"

"Just a minute and I'll be down!"

Elisabeth delayed for a moment in front of the glass, decided that she looked terrible, then took Paula's letter from the mantelpiece, and went downstairs.

"Don't get into a state, my dear: she had to leave, but" – she added immediately – "she won't be away for more than a fortnight. . . . I expect she has explained everything in this letter."

Bob tore open the envelope, took in the contents at a glance, shot a questioning look at Elisabeth, then began to re-read the letter with closer attention. His brows were knitted in a frown: his lips moved as though he were spelling out each word.

"Why did she go? What has happened? Something must have happened . . . what was it?"

"You mustn't look like that: she'll come back: you know what young girls are. She wanted to think, to get matters straight in her mind. Perhaps you may have gone a little too far, yesterday?"

"Do you think that could have been the reason?" (he smiled):
"in that case I've no reason to be uneasy. Nothing's so quickly
forgiven as love-making. Don't you agree?"

Elisabeth felt that she was blushing. Bob ran through the
letter once again.

"Impossible! I know her too well. The fact is she's acted in
obedience to some reason I know nothing of, that she knew
nothing of when she said good-night to me at the front-door.
I remember her last words to me: 'Why shouldn't we wait together and see the dawn?' I made a joke about the lark: you
know the song. I hummed it: 'Ce n'est pas le jour, ce n'est pas
l'alouette . . .' "

"Elisabeth!"

They looked up and saw a frightening vision of old Gornac's
face at a window. He made no reply to Bob's greeting, but
merely groaned.

"Come up at once, my dear: I've got a turn of m'sciatica."

If that were true, Elisabeth would be chained to him for as
long as it lasted. She did not mind the nursing, but she would
have to run endless errands, taking his orders and counter-
orders to the Galberts. She answered calmly:

"That doesn't surprise me. There's been a change in the
weather. You're a living barometer, you know."

"So long as it doesn't hail . . .!"

"Of course it won't hail, father. Don't expose yourself to the
air. I'll come up."

The old man shut the window. Elisabeth said to Bob:

"I'll try to see you again after lunch: during the siesta. Don't
worry: Paula will come back."

He made no reply, but walked away, his eyes on the ground,
chewing a blade of grass. The sky hung low and livid. The oxen
were moving in a cloud of flies.

"There'll be a storm before evening," he said to the herds-
man.

"A little water won't do no harm."

An enormous toad hopped across the path: a sure sign of rain.
Just as Bob reached the terrace he saw Pierre who was wearing
a dark town suit and had his neck encased in a stiff collar. He
showed some surprise, looked up from his book, and seemed at
first about to move away. But, having changed his mind, he
waved a hand just as he might have done had Bob been one of
the farm-workers. Bob had not been thinking of him at all.
True, he had recognized him on the previous evening in the
moonlight, and had taken to his heels, dragging Paula with him
in the direction of the vines. . . . Had Paula perhaps seen him
before going to bed? Had she actually had a talk with that
church-haunting beadle, that nauseating Tartufe? For a moment
Bob was a prey to indecision. He stood where he was, still
chewing his blade of grass.

"Come down to the country for a bit, eh?" Pierre responded
with a nod, and pretended to be immersed in his reading. But
the other had made up his mind that he would not yield an inch
of ground.

"You're unlucky. . . ."

"Oh, it doesn't in the least matter to me whether it rains. . . ."

"I wasn't referring to the weather. . . . I meant that if you'd
arrived a day earlier you'd have met a girl at Viridis."

This time Pierre returned Bob's look. He shut his book, and
said:

"Mademoiselle de la Sesque? – Oh, but I saw her last evening, or, rather, last night. We chattered away, would you
believe it?, until two a.m."

The two young dogs stood bristling at one another.

"I thought as much," said Bob.

"It so happens that we are cousins. . . . She is intelligent . . . one of the rare young women with whom one can converse."

Pierre Gornac lay back in his garden chair, with his legs crossed, swinging one of his feet rhythmically to and fro.

Bob went on:

"So, you were deep in serious subjects until two o'clock?"

"If you don't mind my saying so, I find you somewhat too inquisitive. . . ."

"I suppose what you mean is that *I* am meddling in *your* affairs? It wouldn't be *you*, by any chance, who has been meddling in *mine*? . . . Come now, take that sidelong squint off your face, and look me straight in the eyes."

Pierre jumped to his feet, overturning the chair. Both started to talk at the same moment.

"If you think that being insulted by a man of your sort . . ."

"At least I'm not a Tartufe who *smears* people . . ."

"Would it be possible to smear *you*? . . ."

"Own up, and admit that you've been playing a dirty trick on me with Mademoiselle de la Sesque. . . ."

"She put certain questions to me, and I answered them."

"By what right, may I ask? Do you know me? What do you know of my life?"

"Only what everybody knows."

Pierre felt himself to be in the stronger position. He was risking nothing that mattered to him. He saw his adversary go pale: noticed that the over-red lips were twitching. As the branding-iron, in the old days, marked the shoulders of felons with the ignominious fleur-de-lys, so now did Pierre's provocative words make visible upon the just too handsome face a blemish, a mark of shame.

"No need for you to be uneasy. I informed Mademoiselle de la Sesque, at her request, of certain things that are being said about you. But I should have felt contaminated, I should have feared to contaminate the imagination of a young girl, had I revealed still other horrors of which, I hope wrongly, you are said to be guilty. The people she is going to question, may, perhaps, be less scrupulous. . . ."

He could hit hard: and how badly young Lagave reacted! Each word went home on him like a blow: he reeled under the impact. It amazed Pierre to think that he should have lain awake till dawn, racked with anguish at the thought of what he had done, searching his heart, calling God to witness, deeply disturbed because he had acted in obedience to motives which might, perhaps, have been unworthy of him. . . . He had been terrified at the idea of meeting Paula again. But now, one single glance at this livid face was enough to reassure him. So far as it had been in his power to do, he had saved a young girl, torn her loose from this filthy little creature. Some day she would be grateful to him . . . and, even if she should curse him. . . . Pierre picked up his book: there was nothing more to keep him here. Nevertheless, he hesitated, worried by the dead look in the other's eyes, by the impression of utter collapse conveyed by the manner in which Bob was leaning against the balustrade. What a blow he had dealt him! 'Somehow one never believes that fellows like that are capable of feeling shame. Perhaps I did go a bit too far . . .!' Pierre did not know that his victim had ceased to hear, had ceased to see, him, that there was only one thought in his mind: 'This is the end: she won't come back: I have lost her!' So completely had he forgotten Pierre's presence that he did not even wipe the tears from his cheeks.

Young Gornac saw them. He was deeply touched, even staggered, by the sight. In a flash his whole attitude changed. It took very little to affect his morbidly sensitive heart, his scrupulous spirit. Had he truly reconciled charity with justice? He had lain awake till dawn examining his conscience in this matter, and here, confronted by the tears of the evil-doer, his doubts revived. His bowels of Christian love were moved. A flood of compassion drowned all other feelings in him. His eyes grew soft, his voice honeyed:

"Don't cry . . . it is never too late to mend. . . ."

But Bob appeared to be deaf. His gaze was obstinately fixed upon the gloomy distance, the slate-coloured sky. The West wind brought the sound of church bells, and the rumbling of a train, to where he was standing, a sure heralding, at Viridis, of rain. He stared out over the immense stretch of country which was now soundless and empty.

Pierre drove steadily on:

"Believe me, great happiness may come to you through suffering. You have only to desire it, and it will be granted to you. There is no guilt that cannot be remitted. I acted as I did only for your future happiness, but, admittedly with violence which was as unjust as it was abominable. I ask your forgiveness. I mean that. Forgive me."

'How intently he is listening' – thought Pierre: 'Perhaps I am doing him some good.'

The pleasure he was feeling at this moment was of the sort his kind heart hankered after. He was doing good, and, though now the victor at the very pinnacle of his triumph, was humiliating himself, acknowledging his errors, acquiring merit. But why did not Bob speak:

"Would you like to confide in me, lean on me?"

Suddenly he was conscious of a feeling of deep sympathy for this blighted young life which now, thanks to him, had been made to realize the depths to which it had fallen. He looked at Lagave's hand which was resting motionless on the stone balustrade, a too well-tended hand which had, upon its index finger, a cameo the colour of dried blood – the very hand which Paula once had raised to her lips. Pierre shyly extended his own.

"Give me your hand. Not only shall we no longer be enemies, but I will help you. Yes, I will help you to be worthy. . . ."

The feel of the damp palm woke Bob from his brooding. He violently withdrew his arm and stared at Pierre Gornac as though he had only just realized his presence.

"You!" – he said hoarsely: "you. . . ."

"Don't look at me so furiously. Even yesterday night, even a few moments ago, in spite of my seeming harshness, I was acting for your good. Let me remind you that you have a soul. Ah! that poor soul of yours! No one has ever spoken to you of it. That is why so much less will be demanded of you than of others. *I* love your soul, because in spite of its defilement, it is still beautiful, and shines with a great splendour. I cannot find words in which to describe the compassion that I feel for your soul!"

How well he talked! The tears came into his own eyes. He was moved, deeply moved, by feelings of tenderness and hope. Bob was listening to him, was, as they say, listening with his eyes: he was devouring him with his eyes, and came closer, no doubt in order to hear better. Then, suddenly, he raised his fist.

Pierre Gornac went down under the blow. The cicadas were shrilling round his prostrate body. Blood was trickling from one nostril, and caking on the sparse hairs of his moustache. His mouth, too, was bleeding. One of his lips must have been split, and a tooth knocked out.

Bob did not wait for his enemy to open his eyes. He strode off down the alley, between the hornbeams and the vines, as though following the trail of his vanished happiness. Conscious of a vague sense of relief, he read Paula's letter once more. No, nothing was lost: she would come back: perhaps people wouldn't talk: people aren't, all of them, malicious. Besides, she wouldn't believe them. There was no proof against him. One could always make a flat denial, always say one had been slandered.

The heavy, low-hanging sky was more oppressive than the cloudless blue. Between two rows of vines he went to ground like a hare, facing the dead plain. A scattering of storms rumbled round the vast arena. Yes, deny, deny . . . all the same that did not alter the fact that he had lived his life – a life, certain chapters in which would have made Paula recoil in amazement and horror. But perhaps she would not understand them.

"My life" – he murmured: – "my life . . ."

He was only twenty-three. Which of the many acts which now were beating at the walls of his memory, had he truly willed? Which of them had ever been premeditated? Even before he had learned the nature of what goes by the name of evil, the voices had been numberless which had called, which had solicited him. Around that ignorant body desires and appetites had swirled and eddied. Since childhood he had been hemmed in by a muffled murmur of concupiscence. Ah, no! *he* had not chosen one road rather than another. It had been chosen for him, for a miserable little Tom Thumb lost in the ogres' forest. An angelic face had been his undoing. Angels should never let themselves be seen: woe to angels lost among men! But why, then, should he attach importance to those acts? They had left no mark upon his body.

'I shall write to Paula; I shall say – "I have done nothing and I have done everything – what does it matter? A love like ours covers all: it is a rising tide which does not ebb, but stays for ever at the slack . . ." '

Such were his thoughts as he lay hidden among the vines. Had he succeeded in convincing himself? Do our acts truly leave no trace upon us? Only a few months ago, when someone had asked him how he was going to spend his holidays, he had replied:

"I'm on the look-out for a girl who's got a yacht."

He thought only of his pleasures: of pleasure in general. He demanded of every minute that it should yield its drop of satisfaction. For the moment, love had concentrated all his wayward desires in one single and devouring hunger. But once that hunger should have been assuaged, would they not recover the exigence of every day and every second? What was he but a pet animal trained to eat from many hands.

But this he would not admit, not even to himself. He never doubted for a moment that with Paula in his life, all wretchedness, all dissatisfaction would be wiped out. But she never would be in his life. That he knew, having never believed in happiness. Life without Paula . . . with despairing eyes he measured up the long line of the days to come, as empty as this livid, sleeping plain under a darkened sky, such a sky as might hang above the end of the world, now and again riven by lightning flashes. Into that desert he would have to plunge, there to be devoured by *others*, and, at every moment, conscious that he was just a little less young. At twenty-three he was already suffering: ever since his eighteenth year he had been agonizingly aware that he was growing older. When, on his birthdays, he heard the gratulatory laughter of his friends, and saw their glasses raised in salutation, he had to choke back his tears. Those who loved him knew his face less well than he knew it himself. Each morning he sought in the mirror those signs which, though imperceptible to others, were to him already so familiar: the fine-etched line between nostrils and

mouth; a few white hairs which in spite of plucking he knew
would grow again. Only with Paula beside him could he have
accepted with equanimity the threat of advancing age. He
knew well that, in her eyes, he would be until the end of life,
a child, a sad and sorry child. But now she had turned from him:
he had lost her . . . and all because of that beastly . . . suddenly
he burst out laughing at the memory of that ridiculous puppet
lying broken on the grass. By this time he must have come
round. Why had he not killed him? He hated him so much that
he could genuinely wish, now, at this moment, that he were
dead.

"To have killed him! . . . that would be too good to be true!
. . ." – he said aloud.

True to his rule of life, which was never to resist any impulse,
he let himself be swept forward on a tide of furious enmity.

All around him widely spaced drops were splashing heavily
upon the vine-leaves stained with sulphate. He heard them long
before he felt them on his face or on his hands. The first to
reach him made a star upon his wrist. It was warm, and he
brushed it off with his lips. Then the rain began to fall more
rapidly, mingled with a few hailstones – fairly large ones. But
they did not worry him, because he knew that hail mixed with
rain seldom causes serious damage. He did not move. Water
ran down warm between his shirt and his neck. To be dead is
thus to endure in complete indifference both fire and water, is
to become a *thing*. Things do not suffer. The idea of suffering to
come terrified him. If, for a single moment he thought that his
pain might be tolerable, was that not the reason he still treasured
a tiny hope? He used his hat to shelter Paula's letter so that he
might be able to read it yet again. She would be back, she said,
within a fortnight. A fortnight was the time she asked of him
for reflexion, for getting her thoughts in order. She loved him.

No matter what anyone might say she would come back because she loved him. He spoke her name aloud – "Paula!", and,
since the rain by this time was sputtering on the vines as though
it would never stop, and making so much noise that he was
deafened, he shouted it at the top of his voice. It was a sheer
delight to him to set her name ringing out, dominating the
noises of a chilled, tormented nature.

Suddenly, he remembered his recent illness. He was soaked
to the skin. Whatever happened, he must not be ill again, must
not die until Paula had returned. He ran through the rain in an
effort to keep warm, and, without pausing to take breath,
reached Maria Lagave's house. Contrary to her usual habit, his
grandmother had gone out. Something unforeseen must have
happened to have made her do so in such weather. He threw a
handful of twigs upon the fire: his clothes began to steam. Only
then did he notice on the table a sheet of paper with words
scrawled on it in pencil. He recognized Elisabeth's handwriting:

My dear Maria: M. Gornac has been taken rather seriously
ill. The doctor has just been. He thinks there is no cause for
alarm – but the patient still finds it difficult to speak, and
when he does it is your name that he repeats again and again.
I beg you to come as soon as you can. To add to our troubles,
Pierre has had a fall from the terrace. He has bruised his face,
but there is nothing really wrong with him. Please tell
Bob not on any account to put himself out.

The last sentence was underlined. Pierre must have been
whining to his mother.

'Bah! Madame Gornac will forgive me . . . she has forgiven
me already. . . .'
He could hear his grandmother dropping her clogs noisily on

the doorstep. She came into the house, and, for a moment, her enormous, dripping umbrella filled the aperture of the door.

"You've read her note? They call it an upset: in my opinion it's more like a stroke. The poor man's mouth is all twisted. He was so glad to see me that he cried. I'm going back to sit with him to-night. Madame Prudent gave me this letter for you. Monsieur Pierre's in bed with a poultice on his face. It seems he fell off the terrace . . . fancy his doing that at his age! And then, on top of everything else, the hail! This has been an unlucky day. It wouldn't surprise me to learn as it was the hail as gave the poor old man a turn. He didn't see as it was mixed with rain and wouldn't do much harm. I had a good look on my way over: the grapes haven't been hurt, and the leaves very little. . . ."

Bob read Elisabeth's letter:

You behaved like a young hooligan, though I admit you had some excuse for what you did. I shall have to be with my father-in-law night and day, and no doubt you realize that your presence up here at the house is impossible so long as Pierre is with us, though he has already forgiven you – as he has asked me to make a point of mentioning. My dear boy, I do beg you not to give way to grief. I wrote to you know whom this morning. I expect you have written too. . . .

No, as yet he had not even thought of writing. He dreaded the idea, because she always laughed at his bad spelling. Besides, he would find it difficult to put what he was feeling into words. But perhaps to-day, he might manage to be more eloquent than usual. He went to his room and set to work. Later, Paula was to reproach herself bitterly for not having answered this letter. In it Bob told her all about his quarrel with Pierre. She knew that, from now on, Viridis would no longer be a possible asylum for the young man, that Madame Gornac would be unable to leave her father-in-law's side – in short that there was nobody now within call who could be of the slightest use to him. She had wanted to know about the hidden truths of Bob's life: she wanted to make him uneasy, to put him to the test: she had wanted to punish him. But he was one of those who will never submit to any form of test, nor take any punishment with resignation. He was suffering acutely: if Paula would not even condescend to answer his letter, what madness it had been to count upon her coming back! He was sure now that he would never see her again.

The days passed. The fine weather returned with great heat. Thank God, Maria Lagave scarcely ever left old Gornac's bedside. Bob was free to suffer as much as he liked. Often, at siesta time, when the shutters were closed, he cried and groaned with his head buried in the bolster. Some grain of hope sustained him however, since he had nothing to do but watch the cars passing on the road. He could recognize from a distance the size of each, and, when he heard a ten-horse, rushed regularly downstairs. Drink was also a help. Since he did not want to go far from the house (Paula might turn up at any minute) he bought in Langon some bottles of brandy and kirsch which he drank almost neat. When at last he was well and truly drunk, he lay down in the fly-infested shade, spluttering and singing. He told himself stories, or, rather, as one does with a sick child, beguiled himself with inventing pictures, puerile pictures and, not seldom, obscene. He was filled with pity for the young Lagave, and amazed that nobody came to console him. He would have been only too glad to sleep with his head on any shoulder, and kept on saying, again and again:

"Poor Bob! poor boy!"

Often, too, he was shaken with anger at the thought of the well-beloved:

"What a little fool to think I shouldn't get cured of her!"

He made plans. He would, he thought, drop a line to one or other of his acquaintances. Sooner or later, he'd got to die, to kick the bucket, but meanwhile he would enjoy what time remained to him. . . . With the gift that drunkards have for answering imaginary interlocutors, he would say out loud:

"Lost my reputation, have I? – well, in that case, I'd better get something out of it. Just you see! I'll dam' well show you what happens when you start butting in . . . it won't cost me a penny-piece. . . . I'm proud of it. . . ."

"Who's that you're talking to, Bob?"

He hoisted himself up and saw Elisabeth standing in the doorway.

"How dark it is in here! were you having a siesta? I think you were dreaming, my poor boy, weren't you? I can't come and go as I please, but the patient's dozing, and I told Maria I was going out to get a breath of fresh air. . . . Have you had a letter? . . . No? . . . don't worry: she hasn't written to me either. I'm sure it's because she means to drop in on us unannounced, one of these fine days. . . . But where on earth are you going to see her? Here, I suppose, to some extent, because Maria hardly ever leaves our house now, and in the lanes, of course, or among the vines. . . . That'll take care of itself. But how strange you look, Bob! Why are you staring at me like that, and saying nothing?"

He had got off the bed. She guessed that he must be in his shirt-sleeves, but the shutters kept any light from entering the room.

"I'll open up," she said.

"No, don't: you'll only let the heat in. Come and sit beside me on the bed, Madame Gornac."

"I've only just looked in for a moment, I won't sit down. D'you know, Bob, I scarcely recognize your voice . . . you speak so oddly . . . you're still half asleep, my poor boy!"

"No, no . . . I've given up sleeping . . . I'm going to show you that I don't sleep. . . ."

She had scarcely time to cry out:

"What's the matter with you? you must be out of your mind!"

Suddenly she felt herself seized, held in an embrace. She could smell, close to her face, the alcohol on his hot breath. But so unsteady was Bob on his legs, that she freed herself without difficulty, and sent him reeling back across the bed. He lay there, giggling. Madame Gornac, with her hand on the latch of the door, turned and said:

"I'm not angry with you: you've been drinking."

His voice, when he spoke again, had the note of the gutter.

"You might as well have taken advantage of it . . . you'll be sorry you missed a chance . . . know you will. . . ."

Her only answer was an exclamation of disgust. She slammed the door behind her. Bob could hear her running down the path.

"If y'think I'm going to go prancing after you! . . ."

He laughed to himself. Elisabeth, after crossing the road, entered the sleeping house. The sick-room was silent. She still had a few moments of respite. She went to her room, shot the bolt, flung herself on her bed, and, at last, gave rein to her tears.

IX

NEXT morning, Bob, now sober and thoroughly ashamed of himself, thought of writing a letter of apology. But what was the point in doing that? Paula had been gone now for eighteen days, and nothing else had any importance in his eyes. He didn't care a row of pins what old mother Gornac might think of him. The only thing that would have given him any pleasure would have been to make Paula suffer, to revenge himself on Paula.

"I'll be even with you yet" – he muttered.

He thought that his only reason for wanting her here now was that it would give him the chance of kicking her out. In the stories with which he drugged himself, the girl always now figured as humiliated. He left his room and went through the former kitchen, now transformed into a drawing-room with a door opening into the garden. His grandmother's bedroom held him enthralled for a long time. The whole house was open to him now during Maria's absence in the nearby sickroom. Being at a loose end, he pulled out all the drawers, sampled the sickly-sweet cordials – home-made *eau de noix* and *angélique*, pilfered a pickled onion and a brandy-plum, sniffed the fragrance of vanilla and cloves, as he had done as a child, tried to pick out in the group photographs of the Junior Seminary, spotted all over with dead flies, among forty or so shaven heads grouped round the hollow-cheeked priests, the sickly face and lack-lustre eyes of Augustin Lagave – then, once more, went back to his own room, lay down on the bed and shut his eyes.

He was sleeping deeply when Maria Lagave pushed the front-door ajar and then closed it hastily against the invasion of heat and flies. Madame Prudent had told her that she talked too much and was wearing Monsieur Gornac out. By this she understood that she was in the way. She didn't need to be told that sort of thing twice! – but Madame Prudent would be "properly had" the next time Monsieur asked for Maria. He'd rather have her to look after him than anybody else. She sat down on a low chair in the coolness of the back-kitchen, and began to knit, muttering to herself and brooding over her grievance.

The sound of a car woke Bob. He realized at once that it was a large and powerful car, of no interest to him, and shut his eyes again. But the purr of the engine did not die away. He caught the sound of familiar voices, and rushed down the stairs. Scarcely had he opened the door, dazed by the glare and screwing up his eyes, that he heard his name called by several masked persons in a large car which was covered in dust and stood quivering in front of the house. Maria Lagave, whose presence on the premises was unknown to Bob, had also come out to the road, but ran back into the kitchen when she saw that Bob was bringing these strange monsters into her house. In a furious temper, she held her breath and pressed her ear to the door. But she could make nothing of the prattle. The intruders numbered four: two men and two women.

"We were told it was the first house opposite the château. . . ."

"But everything seemed so hermetically sealed and dead . . . then you appeared in the doorway, like the angel of the resurrection in that picture by . . . by . . . you know the one I mean, princess. . . ."

"Gracious! how peaky he looks! – the fact is, no one's ever well except in Paris . . . just as well face it, everywhere else one just goes to pieces. . . ."

"– Biarritz? – the place is like a tomb. . . . We're making for Deauville in three jumps."

"We've got a nice little bit of dirt for you: did you know Isabelle was getting a divorce: a fantastic business . . . all because of the Russian, of course . . . something to do with her husband: – it seems that . . ."

"Not really?"

"One's pretty tolerant, but there are limits. . . ."

"Oh! what a duck of a bonnet-stand – I adore these peasant interiors: and that perfectly *sweet* chair!"

"And those fire-dogs! they're all the rage now. . . ."

"I expect you've noticed, princess, that the one on the right has a flat top: that's because in the old days, on winter evenings, the nurse, but only the nurse, was allowed to put her plate on it."

". . . And so, the father said to his children – you can choose: either you don't see your mother again, or you don't get a penny from me. . . ."

"And, naturally, they all turned their mother down?"

"How right you are! they say she's dying of grief."

"Oh well, if she does, they'll come into something from her, too."

"The duchess's mother was American or Jewish, wasn't she?"

"American *and* Jewish: – she had the best of both worlds."

"Curiouser and curiouser – all the same, she's very much top-drawer. . . ."

"The husky voice, you mean? that's easily picked up. . . ."

"Husky, my foot! it's a man's voice. . . ."

"If it was only the voice! . . ."

"You don't really mean that? . . . it's the first I've heard of it."

"But it's common knowledge!"

"But I thought she's teamed up with Déodat!"

"Oh, that's ancient history ... and that reminds me ... I suppose you know Déodat's had a stroke? He walks in slow motion now ... it really is most frightfully comic. All the same, he goes on giving parties. .... I'm told his children give an imitation of his ataxia behind his back. ..."

"Oh, but how too beastly!"

"It would be if they *were* his children. ..."

Maria Lagave, with ears pricked, could not understand a word. All the same she knew that some kind of mud was being stirred on the other side of the door. She muttered abuse about the grandson of hers who had thrown open *her* house to a lot of Paris hussies. What were they making such a noise for? What would they find to say next? ...

"Cocktails, here?"

"Why not? – we've got all the necessaries: the shaker's in the car. ..."

"How about ice?"

"Our neighbours opposite, the Gornacs, have got a freezer. I'm well in with the servants ... won't be a moment."

"Ask for some lemons, too, Bob, while you're about it."

Through the cracks in the shutters Maria saw Bob cross the road. A tall young man in his shirtsleeves, hatless, and with his chest bare, was engaged in taking bottles from the car.

"Gin, Vermouth, Angostura ..." he announced, coming back into the house.

They took full advantage of Bob's brief absence.

"He's looking like death. ..."

"But there can't be anyone here to ... to get him into such a state of exhaustion. ..."

Something was said in a low voice, but Maria could not hear what it was. There was a protest from the princess. ...

"Don't be disgusting, Alain!"

"That's the father, over there . . . the enlarged photo. . . .
God! what a mug! Don't you adore the pince-nez, and the
red ribbon? – why it must be pretty nearly as broad as my
hand."

"Bob's had a knock-out, if you ask me. Oh, I don't mean to
say the old charm isn't still there, but . . ."

"Charm at its last gasp . . ."

"The fag-end of a pic-nic . . ."

"Look out! here he is . . ."

Bob's excited voice rang out:

"This'll be enough ice, won't it? – Cocktails! Oh joy!"

"Wait a moment, I'll go and fetch the portable, and we'll put
a record on . . . why of course we always take it with us. When
there's a breakdown we dance to it on the road."

Through the keyhole, Maria could see Bob with his hands
over his head, wildly waving a metal box.

"Which record?"

"*That Certain Feeling*."

"No, the one Bob's so fond of: . . . *Sometimes I'm Happy*."

They were dancing now to what sounded like the music of
savages. When they'd gone Maria would burn some sugar, and
sluice down the tiled floor with water. As to Bob, she'd see to it
that he didn't do this sort of thing again! The nasty young
scamp's voice could be heard over all the others.

The princess said:

"You've had four, Bob, that's quite enough."

"That's because, when you've gone it'll be good-bye to
cocktails!"

"Why not come with us?"

"Tell you what, we'll kidnap you! That's a grand idea. . . .
Remember that night we came out of the *Boeuf*, and started off

for Rouen at two o'clock in the morning, just as we were,
dinner-jackets and pumps?"

"Oh, do, Bob. Deauville'll be much better for you than this
dump. I know you: you can't live without a bit of fun. . . ."

"Just one more drink and I'm your man . . . take you at your
word . . . anything to get away!"

Once more the gramophone began to bray. Maria could
hear the sound of chairs been overturned. Bob called out:

"I must take a dressing-case and shaving-kit: – shan't be a
moment. . . ."

X

H<small>E</small> hadn't even bothered about leaving a letter for his grandmother. Cigarettes were still smouldering in a saucer. Maria thought she could see bloodstains on the cloth, but it was only a squashed lipstick. In spite of the heat she threw the shutters wide. The smell of tobacco and scent made her feel sick.

"Good riddance! Let him get himself hanged, if he likes, but not here!"

If only poor Augustin had not been his father! . . . Ought she to send him a telegram? Though she had sworn not to set foot again in the château, Maria hurried back there, all agog to break the news and talk it over with Madame Prudent – perhaps, too, rather wanting to see what Madame Prudent would look like when she heard.

So far as the half-light in which Monsieur Gornac was dozing allowed her to see anything, she got the impression that Elisabeth was more surprised than agitated. Her face showed nothing, and her voice was perfectly calm.

"You did everything you could, my poor Maria. One can't save people if they won't be saved. . . . Certainly, send a wire to his father: it's for him to decide what steps to take. ... ."

Elisabeth's calmness was not assumed. As soon as Maria had left, she sat in an armchair upholstered in black silk, glanced at the clock to see that it was going properly, listened to the breathing of the man in the bed. She could hear a fly bumbling round the room. Had she been expecting to suffer? She felt herself all over, as after a fall. No, there was an absence of all pain: perhaps, even, she felt lightened by the lifting of a burden.

The young man whose accomplice she had been, who only yesterday had dared ... (she made a face and shook her head), had now, all of a sudden, disappeared. He need no longer cause her any concern. Finished and done with was the foolishness with which, for too long, her thoughts had been occupied. She was back now among the realities of life, was conscious only of a slight sense of humiliation at having played a part in a faintly equivocal adventure, at having been, if only for a moment, an object of concupiscence. . . . What a fool he had made of her! That hoarse voice still echoed in her ears:

"You might as well have taken advantage of it!"

She got up, tip-toed softly to the window, and opened the shutters. The setting sun was turning the sky to red: the vines were drowsing in the distance. She was not feeling sad, but, oh! how empty the countryside seemed all of a sudden. What unknown tide had ebbed from the wide plain, so that it looked to her like the sea-bed, like a vast and empty arena? A cool wind was fluttering the faded leaves. Somewhere it had been raining. She left the shutters open, and, standing there motionless, thought about God. Without having to make any special effort, she considered the theatrical occurrences arranged with such care, in every human life, by an Infinite Being.

'It is Thou, O Lord, who hast wiped the slate clean, and hast freed me from an evil presence.'

She began to pray with a fervour of which she would not have believed herself capable, for, as a rule, her piety was arid, and bereft of consolation. But the hard ground had been softened by a storm. She prayed, and suddenly felt that she was being watched. The old man had his vitreous eyes in their setting of inflamed lids, fixed upon his daughter-in-law.

"I feel rested: the pain has gone. It's not so hot now, is it? If only it would rain, the vines would feel more comfortable."

"You should have told me you weren't asleep. I would have read the paper to you."

"I wasn't in the least bored, my dear. I was looking at the photographs on the wall: my poor father, my poor wife, my two boys. . . . I'm the only one left of that little lot."

He spoke with unusual gravity. This was one of the rare moments in his life when his mind was not filled with business anxieties.

"If I get better . . ."

"Come now, father, you're almost convalescent."

"*If* I get better, I'd like to go back once more to Le Bos, and then to the alms-houses in Langon which I look after. I'd like to see once more the places where I lived as a child, when my father and mother were young and happy, where my two boys spent their holidays. Before going back into the earth. . . ."

"Back to God, you mean."

"Fiddlesticks, my dear."

He stopped speaking, overcome by the drowsiness which was causing the doctor some anxiety, because its return was becoming so frequent. All the same, he heard the bell ringing for dinner.

"Go down; I don't want anything."

Pierre was waiting for her in the dining-room. Did he know that Bob had gone? He glanced furtively at his mother. She asked him how he had been spending the afternoon. He said that he had been working at his essay on Father de Foucauld. They started to converse with a greater ease and fluency than they had done for some time. Not that Elisabeth was paying much attention to what her son was saying. Nevertheless, she was to remember later one of the remarks he made that evening:

"There is something really marvellous about that mission of his among the Touaregs, especially when one thinks of all the other clumsy people working in the mission-field, who do such ill service to the cause they have at heart, and succeed only in making themselves hated. In Islam proper there is nothing to be done beyond praying and enduring. Anyone can do that. . . ."

Always these edifying reflexions! She made a great effort to suppress her feeling of irritation. There must, she thought, be some virtue in this sharp-tempered creature, for him to have foregone all thought of vengeance after being knocked down like that! It made her feel guilty that she could not admire him more. . . . Where was Bob at this moment? She conjured up the picture of an Inn bedroom with rumpled sheets.

The meal drew to its end in silence. Through the open window mother and son could see the oxen moving past in a flood of light from a sun which was now so low that the vines almost hid it from sight.

We believe that some human being has vanished entirely from our life. We roll across the entrance to the tomb where memory lies buried, a stone which bears no epitaph. We go back, with a sense of relief, to the life we knew before it was disturbed. Everything is again as though no stranger had ever entered it. But we do not have it in our power to wipe out every trace. The marks left by one individual on another are eternal, and not with impunity can some other's destiny cross our own. On the morning following the day on which Elisabeth, having learned of young Lagave's departure, had been so happy because she felt no pain, a car, driven by Paula de la Sesque, drew up about four o'clock at the front steps of the Château of Viridis. The news which Elisabeth had heard without turning a hair, she now imparted to Paula in a trembling voice. Her heart was beating as violently as was the girl's. She took Paula into the drawing-room, and at once asked her to give an account of herself, reproaching her for not having kept her word. Why had she delayed so long? A postcard would have been enough to quieten the boy's impatience. She had deliberately driven him to despair. Where could he be reached now? A lot of mad creatures had pounced down on Viridis and taken him away, no one knew where. He had gone. Paula said nothing, but stood with her arms hanging at her sides, and with a sulky look on her face.

"I was waiting for letters from Paris. The last of them reached me only yesterday."

Elisabeth shrugged. What point was there in her asking all these questions? But Paula went on protesting that she had done nothing to be ashamed of. She had expected the worst, but the information she had gathered had been far more awful than she had feared. She had been unfair to Pierre, and begged Madame Gornac to tell him so. The fact of the matter was that Pierre had saved her at the last moment.

"Saved you? – but you have come back, my dear . . . too late, perhaps, still, you *are* here."

The sky was overcast. It was raining on the hills. In the darkened room the two women were watching one another, but to no effect.

"I have come back" – said Paula, who had sat down with her back to the light: "I have come back because I cannot give him up."

"What are you worrying about, then? I don't understand you."

"That is because you belong to another age. I have had to break free from your prejudices, which are those of my mother. But for a girl with whom I struck up a friendship at Arcachon, I very much doubt whether I should have succeeded.
. . ."

She spoke hesitatingly, but with a note of bravado in her voice.

"After all," she said: "why should one give up a young man merely on the ground that he is not worthy to be one's husband? Marriage is one thing, love quite another. . . ."

"Aren't you ashamed of talking like that, my child? I can't bear to hear you taking so outrageous a point of view."

"I speak as I think, madame."

"Was it to make that sort of suggestion to Bob that you came back? If it was, I should feel happy in the knowledge that he is no longer here. Loving you as he does, to the exclusion of all other women, he would lose the last of his illusions. I can hear the way in which he would laugh: 'I set her on a pedestal,' he would say, 'only to realize now that she's worse than any of them! . . .'"

"Oh, come now! I know him a great deal better than you do. He would be delighted to learn that I have 'freed myself from conventional thinking' – as he puts it."

"And I am quite sure that what he loves in you, though he may not know it, is a certain purity, a certain freshness. . . ."

The girl got up and put on her gloves again. They both of them noticed, for the first time, that it was raining, and caught the smell of damp earth.

"Won't you wait until the shower's over?"

"I shall be under cover in the car. . . . You'll let me know if you have any news of him, won't you, madame? – or if he comes back?"

"My answer to that question is – no. You mustn't count on my doing anything of the sort . . . I may have been willing to help an engaged couple . . . but I am not going to get mixed up in an intrigue. . . . Why are you laughing?"

"Because, when I was here last, you were much less straight-laced. You spoke of love as though you knew something about it. . . ."

Elisabeth took her arm, and looked her straight in the eyes:

"What are you insinuating?"

"I am insinuating nothing, nothing at all, madame. I will do you the justice of saying that in all this business you have been wonderfully disinterested. . . . No one could accuse you of having worked for your own ends. All the same . . ."

"All the same, what?"

"Only that, at your age, I imagine, disinterestedness is the only form love can take. . . ."

The blood drained from Elisabeth's face. She had scarcely strength enough to exclaim:

"You must be mad! – please leave this house."

She opened the door.

Paula de la Sesque made no attempt to apologize. She had got rid of something which, for a long time now, she had been dying to say to this old woman. She wouldn't find much difficulty in discovering Bob's whereabouts. She would write a letter and address it to Paris. It would be forwarded from there. . . . The two women scarcely so much as said good-bye. Elisabeth watched the car start off in the rain. Then, she went back into the drawing-room, and listened. But nothing was moving. Monsieur Gornac must be asleep. She sat down close to the window, and spoke aloud:

"What a vile thing to say!"

How still stuck fast in this intrigue she was! Would she ever get it out of her sick mind? Why not? Young Lagave was gone. Paula de la Sesque was gone. Everything would once more become normal. The slate had been washed clean. All she had to do now was to recover the rhythm of her daily existence, of her worries, of her prayers. The immediate necessity was to stop doing nothing. The great thing was to be occupied at every moment of her waking life. She went up to Monsieur Gornac's room. She found him seated, in a dressing-gown, at a table littered with account-books. She told him not to tire himself. He made an impatient gesture like a man who is afraid he will have to start adding up a column of figures all over again. She went back downstairs, once more sat at the window, and opened her basket of mending. Instinctively, she began to make the gestures which had come naturally to her in former days, as though they could automatically produce the quietness of mind, the spiritual somnolence, which had always accompanied them. But in vain. It was not so much that she was suffering as that she was bored. Her life had always seemed to her to be so full: but now, how empty it had become! She, who had been used to saying that she didn't know which way to turn, was amazed to find, all of a sudden, that she had nothing to do.

'I am letting everything slide,' she thought. Maybe, but everything was going as smoothly as in the days when she was for ever superintending the wine-store, the chicken-run, the kitchen and the laundry.

She saw Pierre and the curé, sharing an umbrella, walking towards the house. They were deep in argument. She got up and "made herself scarce", as the phrase went in the Gornac family.

A succession of rainy days followed. No warning came to her. At one moment of one especial night no shock woke her. No vision came to her of men running on a wet road towards an overturned car in flames. She did not hear the screams as of an animal in pain. She did not see, by the light of the blazing wreckage, the bloodstained body, the unrecognizable face, the charred hands.

Once more the sun shone. A light breeze was drying the roads. Monsieur Gornac began to go out again. Pierre avoided him as much as possible, slowly pacing the garden paths, deep in a book. He was wearing the same clothes in the country as he did in town. Sometimes he stopped to make a note.

At last the fatal day dawned. Maria Lagave appeared in the drawing-room after lunch, just as Madame Gornac was pouring out coffee for Pierre. At the sound of the opening door, Monsieur Gornac, who was nodding over a newspaper, raised his old head. Maria, without saying a word, held a letter out to Elisabeth. Not for a single moment, while Madame Prudent was reading it, did her eyes leave her face. In a low voice, Elisabeth said:

"Oh God! how frightful!"

Her hands were trembling. She gave the sheet of paper to her son.

"I can't make out Augustin's writing: Read it, will you. . . . Sit down, my poor Maria."

She moved away from the window and leaned against the wall with the light behind her. Pierre spelled out the letter from Augustin Lagave.

And so, mother dear, all the time I thought he was still with you, he had made off and was rushing round with his wild friends. It appears, from the inquest, that he did not see that the level-crossing was closed, and we can only suppose that he was drunk. According to the speedometer he was doing a hundred and twenty kilometres an hours. A blush of shame suffuses my brow as I write this. The wretched boy

died as he had lived. You and I can take comfort in the knowledge that we had done our duty by him. My life of honourable labour set him an example which he did not follow, but
my conscience is clear. His half-charred remains have been
put into a leaden coffin. Owing to the fact that at this time of
the year many of my seniors and my juniors are away on
holiday there will be only a very short funeral service in
Paris. The Minister has most graciously sent me his con-
dolences, and I am sure that he will be represented at the
ceremony. Though the cost of transport is exorbitant, I have
decided that my son shall be buried at Viridis. I shall arrive,
with the body, on Thursday morning. There is no need for
you to worry about the arrangements. The undertakers will
see to everything. So far I have nothing but praise for the
dignified way in which they have carried out their task. They
are a first-class firm. Their terms, as I have already told you,
are high, but I do not regret this last of my many services to
a boy who never gave me a word of thanks for the sacrifices
I have made on his behalf. I will not attempt to describe
Hortense's grief. I have tried, though in vain, to soften the
blow by telling her that, had he lived, our poor Robert's life
would, at the best, have been a failure. This attitude of mine,
perfectly reasonable though it is, merely irritates her. We can
only bow before a mother's grief, and trust that time will do
its kindly work. The body will be taken from the train at
Langon. Please inform the Gornac family.

                    Yours, in affection and sadness.

Monsieur Gornac got up and embraced Maria.
"Ah, my poor friend: it is not right that the young should go
before us."
"Oh, it is for his mother that we should be feeling. For him,

poor young scamp, it is probably all for the best. He would
never have been any good, and who can say what might have
happened?"

"So sudden a death is terrible," said Pierre. "He can have had
no time in which to make his peace with God. We must say
many prayers for him."

"Those dratted cars!" – exclaimed Monsieur Gornac: "A
hundred and twenty an hour! The sooner him and his likes
get'emselves killed, the better, say I!"

Elisabeth did not utter a word. She moved away from the
wall against which she had been leaning, came back into the
light, and, aft   embracing Maria, sat down on the sofa. Pierre
was walking up and down, making his finger-joints crack. The
level of his anguish began to rise.

"If I had not intervened, the boy would never have gone
away. He would be living now: it is I who am responsible for
his death – a death which caught him before he could repent!"

He left the room, carrying his scruple with him to the bottom
of the garden, as a dog carries a bone. Monsieur Gornac said to
Maria that it would do him good to have a bit of a walk, and
that he would go back with her. The two old people went out
arm-in-arm, he, bent, she, once again upright.

Elisabeth was left alone seated in the drawing-room, motionless, her hands in her lap. When Pierre returned, she was still in
the same place and the same attitude. The young man resumed
his pacing up and down.

"You think that I am responsible, mamma, don't you? It is
a terrible burden to bear! I know, of course, that one must first
consider the intention. My intention was honourable, at least,
it seemed so. . . . That does not alter the fact that poor young
Lagave always got on my nerves. . . . It was a question, no
doubt, of seeing that the girl should know the truth about him.

That, too, was a duty. You are not saying anything, mamma:
does that mean that you condemn me?"

"Certainly not, my boy" – she replied apathetically.

She was rubbing her skirt at the knee. Pierre went on knocking against the furniture, but his talk still flowed on endlessly.
He said that one thought only consoled him: one could do
much for the dead: to the end of his life, in all his Communions,
in all his prayers, Lagave's salvation would take the foremost
place in his special intentions.

There was a short silence before he added:

"Poor young man! I can imagine what the ceremony this
morning, at Saint-Francois-Xavier, in the early September
weather, must have been like. . . ."

He could see in imagination the empty nave, the clergy con-
ducting the service in a hurry. It never so much as occurred to
him that Augustin Lagave, who, foreseeing a small attendance,
had sent out an urgent call to all his seniors and all his juniors
who might happen to be still in Paris, had been overcome with
amazement, some hours before the obsequies were due to begin,
at the sight of so many wreaths and sheaves of flowers – almost
all of them roses, but of every known species. They completely
concealed the coffin. They overflowed into the hall of the flat.
But still they came, and had to be stood against the wall of the
house. They lay, already faded, on the pavement, at the brink
of the gutter, amid all the filth of the street. The undertaker's
men deplored the fact that they had not been forewarned, and
hastily went in search of stretchers. Scarcely any of the offerings
bore cards.

'How widely he was loved!' thought Madame Lagave who
was watching the proceedings in a flood of tears. But she refrained from saying this to Augustin, who was looking very

pale. The smell of the massed flowers was making him feel
more unwell than the sight of the corpse could have done. This
was the last whiff that would ever reach him from that strange
country where an unhappy boy had come by the knowledge of
base passions and simple love. When the procession started, he
heard a woman say:

"It must be some actress. . . ."

Augustin walked, stiffly upright, between the sun-baked
house-fronts. The bumping of the hearse, which he could see
in front of him, made the trailing roses shake. The church, contrary to what he had expected, was far from empty. This, at
first, gave him some satisfaction. But very few were the hands
he was obliged to take. Apart from his colleagues at the
Ministry, most of those present, whom he was seeing now for
the first time, confined their respectful greeting to an inclina-
tion of the head. Many disappeared without moving past the
family.

"What are you thinking about, mamma?"

Elisabeth gave a start, and, as though caught doing something
she should not have done, got to her feet.

"Nothing, darling . . . or only about what you said . . . *of
course* you acted in accordance with your conscience."

The tone of her voice was quite neutral. When Pierre suggested that they should go together to the church, she raised no
objection, put on her hat and her gloves and fetched her sun-
shade. They went by way of a footpath which led through
orchards and vineyards, but not a word passed between them.
The Viridis church was dark. Pierre knelt down and hid his
face in his hands. She, too, on her knees gazed fixedly at the
altar, but her lips did not move. Her eyebrows were drawn together in a frown which gave her a hard look, such as no one,

probably, had ever seen upon that placid countenance. She stared at the tabernacle and at the black Virgin decked out in a scarlet, gold-fringed robe, which stood above it. The ticking of the clock sounded loud in the lonely emptiness. As when he was a child, Pierre sat back in his chair with an enquiring look, as though asking her whether she had finished her act of silent worship. She got up, and he followed her. She took some of the holy water which he offered her, but did not cross herself. Outside, in the fading light of the lovely day, they agreed that the evenings were growing cooler. Pierre said that only a week ago they would not have been able to walk as far as the church and back. And so they took their way, talking of indifferent matters. The young man said that perhaps they ought to pay a call on Maria.

"I think it would be the proper thing to do."

She refused in so uncompromising a manner that he was at first surprised.

The evening passed as usual. There was nothing strange in Elisabeth's behaviour, except, perhaps, that she did not have recourse to her work, but sat, as she was accustomed to do on Sunday evenings, with her hands lying idly in her lap. Old Gornac had fallen asleep in the act of reading his paper. Through the open window came the sound of Pierre's footsteps as he paced the garden path: doubtless, he was chewing over his scruples, and brooding on his doubtful thoughts about the death of young Lagave. Perhaps he was thinking of the day and the night, still so close in time, when, in the same grass where the cicadas ceased to scrape at his approach, a head, now cold in death, had rested on the breast of a young and happy girl; a head now forever cold, and a hand which had bruised Pierre's face, for ever motionless. He could not altogether stifle a secret sense of satisfaction: the man who had struck him was no longer

of this world. 'I convinced myself that I had pardoned him! I
had assumed the attitude of pardon, made the gesture of mercy,
but no movement of my heart responded to it. Christianity is
for me no more than an outer covering, a disguise. Even my
passions it does scarcely more than distort. They live, masked
by faith it is true, but, still, they live.' The practical good sense
of those who are addicted to the spiritual life led Pierre to turn
this discovery to account, to transform it into food for his
humility. It is so difficult for the Christian not to think that he
is better than other men! Pierre drove himself on to take the full
measure of his hideous joy at Bob's death. Motionless under the
black elms, he turned his fury against himself, took pleasure in
self-denigration: 'Bob was worth more than I am: he, at least,
wore no mask.' He found a heady delight in his certainty that
he was the lowest of the low, but rejoiced, too, that this knowledge, by itself, made for his spiritual advancement. To those
who live in God, everything has its uses.

The Gornac family retired for the night at the usual hour.
Elisabeth, when she had bolted her door, remained as unmoved
as she had been in the presence of her father-in-law and of her
son. She went to the window, leaned out into the darkness, and
said aloud:
"He is dead. . . ."
But the words awoke no echo in her. The candle scarcely lit
the enormous room. She pressed her forehead to the mirror set
in the wardrobe door, then studied her reflexion attentively.
Speaking to the fat, pale, respectable woman who looked back
at her, she said again, in a colourless voice:
"He is dead . . . dead . . . dead."
She did not say her prayers. She lay down in the darkness.
She dozed: she awoke: she spoke to Bob:

"She's no better, you know, than the others. She'll never marry you!"

She gave a mocking laugh. She thought she was asleep, but could hear the rustling of leaves, the unbroken murmur of the countryside.

XI

ABOUT nine o'clock the next morning, Pierre joined Madame Gornac in the drawing-room, and told her that the Lagave family had arrived at Maria's house. He had just walked there with his grandfather, who said not to wait lunch for him, because he intended to stay with Augustin until the evening. The body had also arrived, and had been laid in the church at Langon. There would be no ceremony at Viridis.

"What body?" she asked.

"Mother dear, young Lagave's."

"The body of young Lagave?"

Pierre took his mother's face between his hands, and looked at her anxiously.

"What are you thinking of, mamma?"

"Nothing. . . ."

"Your thoughts are elsewhere, aren't they? Listen to me: it would be only decent on our part to go and pray by the coffin. It seems that Madame Lagave has refused to leave it. On our way home we will pay our call on Maria."

He spoke with a strange briskness, as though he had been, all at once, relieved of all his scruples. His mother made a sign that she agreed to his suggestion, and he gave instructions that the victoria should be got ready. Scarcely had he taken his seat beside her than he said very quickly:

"I have a piece of news which will make you as happy as it does me. . . . Robert did not die at once. Augustin told me so, though he seems to attach no importance to it."

"He's not dead?"

"He lingered for more than two hours. He knew that he was

dying. A quarter of an hour before the end his mind was perfectly clear. He was taken into the nearest house . . . and what
house do you think that was? . . . the presbytery, as though
quite by chance. He died in the arms of a poor country curé,
who has written a wonderful letter to his parents. Augustin
made me read it. It contained this passage. 'Your son rendered
up his soul with feelings of repentance and of faith . . . glad to
suffer and to die. . . .' God is good, mamma! . . . See how
everything has turned out for the best."

He took his mother's hand and pressed it. Seeing that she did
not stir, but that her lips were moving, he thought that she was
praying and respected her meditation. It gave him happiness to
feel such joy in the fact that the salvation of his enemy was now
assured. He no longer doubted that he had been its most unworthy instrument.

The afternoon sky was leaden, the air heavy: but no storm
broke. It would not rain now. The dust which sullied the road-
side grass was powerless to lay its mark upon the vines which
were already stained with sulphate. The victoria drove down the
hill towards the Garonne. Pierre, unable to keep still, sat rubbing his hands together, and passing them over his face.

"It's odd," he said: "I can still feel the scars where he hit me."

He saw his mother's broad, pale face turn towards him. For
the first time for two days she looked at him with awareness.
She took off one of her gloves. She raised a small, plump hand
and touched each bruise, as though by so doing she were com-
pleting its cure. Then the hand dropped to her side. But she
seemed now to be less spellbound. Her breast rose and fell. She
let her gaze wander over the dark plain. It was the time of year
when, the heavy work over, the men relax and leave the grapes
to ripen in the sun. The country lay all about them empty and

fulfilled, a sea-bed from which someone had withdrawn for ever. The horse crossed the bed of the Garonne at a walking pace. Pierre said:

"How low the water is."

The church at Langon stands close to the bridge. Madame Gornac said what she always said:

"Put the horse in the shade."

They entered the dark and ice-cold nave. Pierre took his mother's arm.

"The right-hand aisle," he said in a low voice.

She followed him. A long object under a piece of black drapery, stood on two trestles. Close to it was a human figure, clad from head to foot in crape. It was Bob's mother, so bent that her forehead almost touched her knees. Pierre, kneeling, was surprised to see that Elisabeth was still standing, her two hands gripping the back of a chair, her lower jaw slightly pendent. Then, suddenly, he heard a long-drawn rattle in her throat, and saw that she was trembling all over. Her shoulders were twitching. She was breathless, and shaken by hiccups. She stayed like this until, at last, her body collapsed upon a chair, as under a rain of blows. The empty church echoed back her heavy sobbing. She made no attempt to wipe the tears from her cheeks, but, one damp hand had disarranged her neat strands of hair. A single loose grey lock gave her an appearance of disarray and shame. In vain did Pierre tell her to lean upon his arm, and go with him. She seemed neither to hear nor to see. Thank God, there was nobody in the church but the dead man and the prostrate, shadowed figure keeping watch beside him. It did not turn its head. But at any moment now, somebody might come in.

"Come with me, mamma: let us not stay here."

But, deaf to his voice, she half stretched her arm towards the coffin, stammering broken words, calling upon the mortal remains lying there before her.

"You are there! It is you who are there!" she said over and over again.

Pierre gave up trying to lead her away. With teeth clenched he waited for the agony to end. This trembling woman was his mother. He prayed. She looked like an old and wounded animal, stretched on its flank and panting – but already less noisily. Anyone might have entered now, and he would have felt no shame. As after thunder the falling rain is audible, only gasps and sighs gave evidence of her terrible grief, and the urgent tears, more numerous in these few brief minutes than all that she had ever shed in the whole course of her life. Seeing that she was calmer now, Pierre went out and told the coachman to lower the hood. Madame, he said, was not feeling very well, was suffering from one of those headaches with which her domestic staff were familiar. Then he went back to his mother, wiped her eyes with a handkerchief dipped in holy water, led her out, and pushed her into the carriage. There was no one at the door, and the coachman (engaged for the summer only) scarcely turned in his seat upon the box.

Shudders were still agitating her body, but she had stopped crying. Pierre could scarcely recognize her. Her cheeks looked hollow: her chin seemed to have grown longer, and livid circles made her eyes appear unusually large. She pushed him away from her, and he thought it was because she still held him guilty of the boy's death. But she was keeping him at a distance as she would have done any other living person. From this pro-found disruption of all her being there emerged now into the light of day a love which lay buried in her flesh, which she had carried within her, like a pregnant woman who does not know at first that she is bearing in her womb a living seed. Because of

the long climb to Viridis, the horse had slowed down. Once
more she began to cry, remembering how, one day, when Bob
was still a child, she had seen him at this very spot. He had been
on his way home from the river, carrying his minute, wet
bathing shorts in his hand, and biting a black grape. Pierre
dared not look at her. How horrible life was! He could bear no
more.

"There is none but Thee, O Lord. From now on I would
know Thee alone."

A sob from his mother made him open his eyes again. Seized
by a spasm of pity, he tried to console her. She must remember,
he said, how young Lagave had died. His salvation now was
certain: the labourer of the eleventh hour, the prodigal son, the
sheep lost and found, the publican, such a one as God loved
best among all His creatures. But she shook her head. She knew
nothing of the soul. Bob, for her, was face and hair and eyes, a
chest which she had seen bared, arms which once he had spread
for her. She turned her face away and leaned it against the
leather of the hood, fearful lest Pierre should read what she was
thinking, in her eyes.

"Those arms he spread for me one day. . . ."

Pierre did not hear the words. Nevertheless, he said:

"We believe in the resurrection of the body."

Once again he saw her turn her ravaged face to him:

"Spare me your sermons."

Could this be his mother, his pious mother, who had
spoken? He realized at last why it was that the faith they held
in common had never formed a bond between them. He felt
nothing but contempt for the sort of old-wives' religion which
does not move the heart: a mixture of personal hygiene and an
insurance policy against the risk of hell-fire – not one rule of
which would Elisabeth ever violate, a meagre concern to keep

on the right side of an eternal busybody, as one might of the Tax Collector – could such a poor hoard count for more than a twig in a tidal wave?

She muttered:

"I have lived: Oh yes, I have lived my life, a life of adding figures, and still more figures. . . ."

Suddenly her eyes met his, and she uttered a groan.

"I feel ashamed in your presence: you cannot know how terribly ashamed!"

He drew her head down on his shoulder. She made no resistance, but closed her eyes and said no more. He remembered having seen her, while she was still a young woman, in the dining-room at Le Bos, sitting with ledgers open before her on the table, and her father-in-law with a pair of tortoise-shell spectacles on his beaky nose, leaning over her. . . . He tried to see in her features, as he had known them in those far distant days, some forewarning of the woman who now sat sobbing and groaning at his side. But he could conjure up nothing but the memory of sudden violent displays of temper, outbursts of quick fury, which made Monsieur Gornac say that his daughter-in-law was like "milk on the boil" – of preferences, too, and antipathies, both utterly irrational. Whether it was a new curé, a vicar, a tenant-farmer, or a domestic servant, she would be "all over" them for a few days, and then, for some trifling matter, would banish them for ever from her favour. But all that meant nothing. Besides, what do we know of the woman who brought us into the world? No flesh is more a mystery to us than that from which our own has drawn its substance. What had his mother been like at the Convent? What had she been like as a young girl? Doubtless, the strictness of school discipline and of her life at home, had turned her out to the pattern of her companions, of all the women of her family, of those who, before ever she had appeared upon the scene, had lived lives of boredom in small and gloomy country towns. But no: however constructing the conditions of a life may be, they do not altogether stifle the heart. Pierre should have considered those grains of wheat discovered in sarcophagi, of which it is said, that, even after five thousand years, they germinate and ripen.

He helped his mother out of the carriage, and, when they were in the hall, said:

"Remember, mamma, that you must go and see the Lagaves at Maria's. Are you in a fit state to pay a call upon the family?"

She straightened up. He had found the one thing to say which could still have an effect upon her. It was her duty to make a visit of condolence to the family. She asked Pierre to go on before her, saying that she would follow in half an hour.

"I shall be all right: don't worry. The blow has fallen: the worst is over."

But he preferred to wait for her. He could hear her moving about in her room over the hall. When she came down again, perfectly correct, already wearing her black gloves, and with her forehead showing pale under the tidily arranged hair, he heaved a sigh of relief. Her eyelids were still red, but nobody would be surprised to see that she had been crying, so well was the kindness of her heart known to all. Besides, the circumstances demanded that all the shutters in Maria's house should be closed. There would be no tell-tale evidence upon her face.

In the drawing-room at the Lagave house, where the members of the family were seated in a circle, Pierre felt frightened when he heard Maria say to Madame Prudent that she had found several handkerchiefs in Bob's wardrobe marked with an "E".

"He must have borrowed them from you the day his nose bled so badly. Would you like to come and see?"

Elisabeth got up, left the whispering group, and with a firm step went up to the bedroom. With its pale-coloured walls the place looked like an empty sepulchre. Motes of dust were dancing in the rays of sunlight which streamed through the cracks in the shutters. It might have been compared to one of those diaphanous chrysalises from which a cicada has taken flight. The sheets had been stripped from the bed, and the bolster was lying against the wall where once a heavy head had rested. The door of the wardrobe creaked. A tie was still hanging inside. Elisabeth's eyes never left the bed. Two arms were stretched towards her, and she could see a thin and wasted face. She remembered the cheek-bones and the over-prominent jaw, the hollow eyes, the tight-drawn skin – a death's-head even in life.

"Yes, they are mine: I recognize them."

She took the handkerchiefs, and, while Maria led the way back to the drawing-room, could, for one brief moment, smell the mingled scent of tobacco and eau-de-Cologne, which came from them. She resumed her seat.

Pierre made his mother promise that after the church service she would not go on to the cemetery. It would be considered only natural that she should stay with Madame Augustin Lagave. She would be free to mingle her tears with those of the poor dead boy's mother. That evening, after dinner, when Monsieur Gornac had gone to his room, she seemed to Pierre to be so calm that he ventured to touch on the burning topic, and confessed that he had written to Mademoiselle de la Sesque. Unless the girl had read the Paris papers she might still be in complete ignorance of what had happened. . . . But Elisabeth, suddenly shaken by a storm of anger, turned on him. What business had he to meddle? – why this mania for intru ding into the lives of others? Didn't he know to his cost the damage he had already done? Wasn't it enough that he should pray for them, since he could never help wanting others to be different from what they were, could never resist the temptation to change, to transform, them?

"If you have written suggesting that she should come here, I give you fair warning that I shall show her the door. I could not endure the presence under my roof of the woman who was the cause of his death."

"But, mamma, you know perfectly well that it was I who . . ."

"It was open to her not to have gone, or, once gone, to have come back. . . . Oh, I know beyond all doubt that you, too, are responsible . . . and I, as well, for I might have got up that morning and warned Bob, so that he could have kept the little fool from running away. . . . But I slept on, I slept on. I do not remember having ever slept so soundly as I did that night."

She said no more, but sat there with the tears pouring down her cheeks. Pierre wandered about the room, disarranging the chairs, talking about God's will, urging his mother to consider with adoration the designs of Providence, and alluding to young Lagave's Christian death. But all she said to him was: –

"Has God made a confidant of you? Of one thing only can we be sure, that his body is in the earth, is rotting; that no eyes will ever see him again, that no hand will touch him. That is all we know for certain. Everything else . . ."

"How can you utter such blasphemy, mamma? It might be grandpapa speaking. . . ."

She protested that blasphemy was far from her intention.

"I know no more . . . I know only that I am in torment." And, in a low voice, she repeated:

". . . in torment . . . in torment . . ."

Pierre, however, wrote out a telegram to Mademoiselle de la Sesque, telling her not to come to Viridis. He took it down to Galbert, and asked him to send it off next morning as soon as the post-office was open. When he got back to the house his mother appeared to be dozing. He opened the window. He could smell the great vat which was being got ready for the grape-harvest. He asked Elisabeth whether she would join with him in saying the evening prayer. But she shook her head in silence. Then, moving a little way from the lamp, he knelt down alone, his elbows on the seat of an armchair, his face buried in his hands. When he got up he saw that his mother had left the room without kissing him good-night.

He got up at dawn and had to walk through a dense fog to early Mass. Sparrows were chirping, but he could not see them. On leaving the church, he followed a path which led him away from the house. The mist was thinning. The smell of the wine-presses awoke in him the memory of autumn holidays. As he walked along the deserted path, he talked to himself. He was strong in his determination to leave at once without a back-ward glance. He was impatient to see his director, in Paris, that he might get him to consent to a shortening of the time which must otherwise elapse before he could separate himself entirely from the world. Bob's salvation was assured, and he could think of him now with undisturbed tenderness. All of his life, all that remained to him of life, should be offered in exchange for the eternal peace of the young man whom he had insulted, whose death he had precipitated – but only death had been able to restore life to that angel of the flesh.

So completely was he absorbed in these thoughts that he found himself once more in front of the house without knowing how he had got there. The first thing he saw was a car drawn up by the front steps. Paula de la Sesque had arrived. His telegram had failed to reach her. She had left Arcachon yesterday, and must have spent the night at Langon. Remembering his mother's threat, he felt badly shaken. What sort of a greeting had she extended to the poor child? He opened the front door but could not summon up sufficient courage to enter the house, and shut it again. No, he could not face Paula. He crept up to the half-opened window of the drawing-room. No sound of voices reached him, and he ventured on a furtive peep. Paula, her back to the window, was seated on the arm of a chair, with her head resting on Elisabeth's shoulder. Pierre could see his mother's hand stroking the girl's hair. Now and again, the other hand moved down her neck and her bare arm, as though she were searching for some trace. She was holding in an embrace the body for which the young Lagave had lived, and now, had died. Her lips moved from palm to wrist, and came to a stop at the inner side of the elbow. Maybe, Elisabeth was moved by an obscure desire to follow some track on the young body, and, like a traveller coming on the burned out ashes of an abandoned camp, pause awhile at the mark of teeth.

Pierre moved away from the window, reached the terrace, and sat down with his legs dangling, as Bob so often had done. He saw, with the eyes of the spirit, God fastened with three nails, motionless upon the cross, incapable of doing anything for men save shed his blood. Thus must His true disciples do: intervening only by the way of sacrifice and blood-offering. One can change nothing in human-beings, nor can human-beings change themselves unless it be by the Creator's will operating in each one of them. They must be ransomed as they are, with all their load of propensities and vices: they must be taken, ravished, saved, with all their sins still on them. All one can do is bleed and obliterate oneself for them.

The young man of twenty-two, seated on the terrace, did not ask himself whether or no his mother might have bequeathed to him any of that passion which had surged up in her after slumbering for so many years. Human-beings do not change: but they may live for a long time without knowing themselves: many die before they ever come by such knowledge, because God, from their earliest age, has kept the evil seed from growing: because He is free to draw unto Himself some of the wildness which, in one or other of their forbears was, perhaps, criminal, and may become so again in their own sons.

He heard Paula's car drive away: he saw it on the road between the trees, and watched it descend the hill into Langon. For as long as possible he followed with his eyes the dust which it had raised, and imagined her drawing up beside the cemetery. He could fancy her walking through the porch where the bier was housed, walking along the cinder path, spelling out the epitaphs, and coming, at last, to the Lagave tomb which immediately adjoined that of the Gornacs (even in death they were not divided). Waggons would be bumping along beyond the wall, on the road to Villandraut, a locomotive puffing, sawmills sounding that endless complaint of theirs which is at once both musical and ear-splitting. Not at this parting of the ways, thought Pierre, would *he* await the resurrection. With his inner eye he saw his light and fragile bones mingling their dust with the desert sand. He must go away from here . . . but was it not his duty to stay with his mother? He was under no illusion about the comfort which his presence might bring to her. He remembered how, as a child, he had felt for her a jealous and a painful love. With her it has been as with all the others he had cherished. Always, in his relations with his fellows, he had been the one who loved rather than the one to whom love was given. Such hearts as his, eternally frustrated, are, in this world, marked out to be God's prey. In his own hand, he had written on the first page of his private journal, the words which Pascal had heard Christ speak to him:

"Other friends you have, but I am more than them, more than ever they could be, because I have done for you what they could never do, nor could they suffer at your hands what I have suffered, nor die for you in the days of your infidelity and cruelty. . . . I love you more ardently than you have ever loved your sins."

More than others, more than that indifferent mother who, through all his life, had shed fewer tears for him than, in the last few days, she had shed for the dead body of a boy who was not hers.

XII

THE course of events delayed the explanation which Pierre wanted to have with his mother. In the first days of the harvest, Monsieur Gornac had another slight stroke. Since Maria was kept busy with her vines, Elisabeth was for ever on the run between the sick-room, the vat, and the wine-store. Pierre offered to help her, but she jumped down his throat with the same show of contempt that she had felt for her timid husband: it was no business of his, she said: in all practical matters he was useless:

"Stick to your books, and, for Heaven's sake, don't meddle!"

He rejoiced to see her once again caught up in the movement of life. Perhaps, unknown to himself, he felt some scorn of her. The great grief had yielded to the urgency of gathering grapes! She was haunted by a fear that Galbert might rob her, and was strict in her accounting of the number of hours put in by the day-labourers. For Pierre she was again as she had always been.

But he saw very little of her. Worn out at the day's end, she went to bed almost before dinner was over. (A nun from the Hospice came each evening from Langon to sit with Monsieur Gornac.) Only once, when Pierre, on his way to bed, and walking on tip-toe past her room, believing her to be asleep, did he think he heard the sound of sighs and sobs. He stopped and listened. The night was filled with rain and wild with wind. Water was running down the panes of the corridor windows and on the roof-tiles to an accompaniment of gurgling gutters. It was difficult to distinguish the sound of human grief from nature's universal wail. Next morning, her look of calmness and preoccupation reassured him. He thought that what he had heard had been but the moaning of the autumn night.

But this preoccupation of hers was also what kept him from speaking about his vocation. Though he felt no doubt that she could do easily without his presence, he was afraid that she might grieve when she knew that he meant to renounce his inheritance, and so lose interest in the land which would one day pass into the hands of strangers. October was almost at an end before he could bring himself to tell her of his plans. It was she, one evening, as she sat drying her muddy boots before the drawing-room fire, who asked him how much longer he meant to stay at Viridis. He replied that he did not like the idea of leaving her alone. She thought he was referring to the harvest, to Monsieur Gornac's illness, and hurt his feelings by saying:

"Oh, if it comes to that, you're not much use to me."

To this he answered that what he had in mind was a longer separation than any she anticipated, and alluded to an invincible attraction, an inner call, to which, in the long run, he would have to hearken. He tried to make out from the look upon her face what effect his words had had upon her. But Elisabeth kept her eyes fixed on the fire, and no sign of disturbance was visible on her face in the bright glow of the logs.

"I have always known that you would go that road," she said at last: "it would have been a tragedy for your grandfather to see you take the habit, but he is sinking a little deeper every day, and will not last out the winter. There can be no point in saying anything to him. It is better that we should let him die in peace."

She asked him whether he intended to enter a seminary or a monastery. Pierre had not yet made up his mind, but, no doubt, he would first make a long retreat in a Trappist house. The thought of Africa greatly appealed to him. As he said this, his throat contracted, because he had a feeling that he was speaking to somebody who was not there. He could not have felt more utterly alone if the drawing-room had been empty, and this woman, his mother, not seated opposite to him, bending over the fire.

"So you approve, mamma?"

"Approve? You are doing what you think is best for your happiness, my poor boy."

Those words, "my poor boy", came to him like a drop of cold water to a man dying of thirst. He looked hard at his mother's face, hoping to see tears in her eyes. But there were none. How he wished that she would cry! And now, he, who at first, had thought only of taking her mind from the thought that one day the estate must be given up, was now the first to mention the subject, so urgently did he want her to suffer. But she interrupted him with a comment which left him speechless:

"Why do you think I should mind? You cannot really believe that it is a matter of the slightest importance to me?"

"But don't you realize, mamma, that when you are dead everything will have to be sold? I shall have taken the vow of poverty. I don't wish to keep a penny. The pines which have always been in the family, the vines which grandpapa planted. . . ."

He had never before worried about these things, but now the spirit of the family was so strong in him that he spoke with as much love as Monsieur Gornac would have done, of all this land of theirs, at the very moment of abandoning, of betraying it. But Elisabeth's detachment remained unaltered:

"If it hadn't been you, it would have been your son or your grandson . . . nothing endures . . . nothing exists. . . ."

She repeated, almost in a whisper:

"Nothing . . . nothing . . . nothing. . . ."

Then Pierre left his chair, sat at his mother's feet, and, as when he was a child, laid his head in her lap. He took one of her passive, withered hands and forced it to lie upon his forehead.

He said that he would be going away for a long time, perhaps for ever. If, sooner or later, he should have to take ship, she would be able to come to see him. But now was the last time in this world that they would ever be living in close propinquity, under this roof, in this old drawing-room, as mother and son. They would never more be together here below. What a wrench for a clumsy-fisted son who never seemed to manage not to get on her nerves, who had never known how to explain how much he loved her.

Now, at long last, her heart was really touched. She cried, she bent her head, and her lips sought the thin, tormented face of the young man whom no human-being, but only God, had chosen. She cried: but the dead man to whom her nightly tears were given, was part cause of these tears, too. Our grief follows always the same slope, flows always to the same being, even when it has first been aroused by another. Elisabeth was sobbing, now, but already she no longer knew whose head it was that lay upon her knees. The rending torment of eternal separation kept her feelings from responding to her own son's coming absence. She kept on saying, as one might in a dream to somebody who is not there: "My child, my poor, poor child!"

Pierre got to his feet, consoled. Thus they stayed together, holding hands but saying nothing: he, feeling certain that now at last, this evening, he had achieved union with his mother: she, listening only to the rain whispering on the cold earth. In thought she could see a stone on which no name had yet been carved, running with water. She imagined the nocturnal solitude of the place, of the withered wreaths. She forced herself to violate the dark secrecy of the grave, stretched herself there in spirit, embraced the body that was lost to her, and let herself be swallowed in that nothingness.

Pierre left Viridis shortly after All Souls' Day. Monsieur Gornac died in December. He had consented to receive the curé in consideration of his daughter-in-law's reiterated wishes. He was not wholly convinced that everything in the teaching of the Church was false. If the Sacraments could do no good, it was unlikely that they would do much harm. Maria Lagave, who, at the end of harvest-time, had slipped and fallen at her washtub and broken a thigh, outlived him by only a few weeks. Augustin Lagave, unable to leave Paris, was glad to lease his property to Elisabeth. She often visited the dead and empty house, and lit fires of vine-shoots in the room where Bob had lived. She soon exhausted all that he had left of himself within those walls, and suffered because she could no longer feel anything there but boredom. Her religious habits one by one came back to her. Her love turned into a matter of scruple. It was some time before she dared to make open admission of it, and was amazed to find that her confessor – a Marist priest from Viridis – did not regard her as an incomprehensible monster.

"You are all the same, my poor daughter," he said: "when one knows one, one knows the lot."

She was surprised to find that her case was in no way an unusual one. Her love became a poorer thing once the special qualities with which she had formerly endowed it were taken away. The Father was careful not to forbid her to think about the dead man, provided she did so in the sight of God. In this way did she domesticate Bob's memory, so that it took its place among her daily throng of special intentions. The slump in wine prices caused her much concern. Though she was very rich, she was worried by the amount of money that Viridis "swallowed up". Not for the world would she have consented to sell out any of her capital. The property must be kept going out of income. This state of affairs she called being "embarrassed". She never spoke to a soul, and was quite incapable of taking an interest in other people's concerns, nor were the details she gave of her own of a kind to thrill her neighbours. The notables of Viridis and Langon paid her one visit a year which she religiously returned. Elisabeth Gornac had the reputation of being miserly, though she subscribed to all the "good works" of the parish.

A morning came when she scarcely took the trouble to read a card which reached her announcing the marriage of Paula de la Sesque with a rich Bazas landowner. She tore it into little pieces, not with any feeling of hatred, but because she was afraid of waking up, of being shaken out of her state of unawareness.

The thought that her properties would be sold after her death did not make her lose interest in them. Perhaps she even felt an obscure satisfaction in the knowledge that Pierre had renounced his rights in advance. She spent three Spring days with him at Marseille, prior to his embarkation. Though he had not assumed the habit, his threadbare clothes, his tie, his shoes were those of a man for whom the visible world no longer existed. On their first day together they felt embarrassed because they had nothing to say to one another, but, later, they grew resigned to silence, and waited in peace of mind for the moment of farewell. Pierre believed in a world where beings would have all eternity in which to know each other. He no longer tried to find out what his mother's placid face and unseeing eyes were hiding. She cried as she stood on the pier while the steamer dropped her moorings, but felt perfectly happy in the train which took her back to Langon. It was the season at which the heavy work begins on the farms, and she was in a hurry to be at home. The vines flowered: the grapes ripened: the harvest was gathered. Elisabeth's life moved to the rhythm of the waxing and the waning year. The rain, the snow, the frost, the sun became her enemies or friends according as they damaged or aided her fortune. Her body announced, far ahead, by aches and pains, the coming changes in the weather.

Fatty degeneration hindered the action of her heart. She moved less and less from home, except to go to Le Bos. It was said in the neighbourhood that Galbert was cheating her. Anonymous letters for a brief while disturbed her peace of mind, but she preferred to pretend that she knew nothing. She complained of Pierre, who never wrote unless to ask for money: as though *she* hadn't got *her* charities!

One summer's day she got out of the victoria in front of a pastry-cook's shop on the Place Maubec, at Langon. A stationary car was quivering at the kerb. A young woman, rather too well-dressed, and somewhat plump, was sharing out cakes among four children. Elisabeth recognized Paula, who turned her face away. The old lady chose a tart and went back to the carriage. She told the driver to stop at the cemetery. She passed through the porch where the bier is housed, walked along the cinder-path, spelling out the epitaphs. She knelt upon the stone which covered her own dead, but not on that which lay above the mortal remains of young Lagave, at which she gazed for a long time, motionless. She noticed that the rail round the grave

needed repainting. Swallows were singing in the blue. A wag-
gon was bumping along the Villandraut road. The sawmills
were keeping up a ceaseless whine. Piles of planks were scent-
ing the afternoon with the smell of fresh resin and shavings. A
locomotive puffed along the track and smudged the cloudless
sky. Two women were talking in patois on the other side of the
wall. A lizard – one of the kind that warmed themselves upon
the terrace at Viridis – half concealed the name of Robert
Lagave, and the date of his birth. It was a summer's day like
thousands of other summer days; like those which would bring
warmth to this stone long after Madame Prudent should have
joined all the other Gornacs who had preceded her in this patch
of ground. A sudden spasm of distress, which came from very
far away, rose in her and filled her being. Ah! she was not yet
so wholly dead as these were! She half closed her eyes, and saw
again a darkened and diaphanous room where young Lagave
stretched arms to her, his teeth glinting, his chest bare. She went
up to the railing which needed repainting, leaned her face
against the bars, and imagined to herself the unplumbed darkness, a sealed box, a scrap of winding-sheet, a fragile scattering of bones. Then at last she knelt. The *De Profundis*
several times repeated, brought order into her grief, nursed
it and kept it regulated. One part of her grew once more
numbed and still. God, who, for her son Pierre, was Spirit and
Life, in her was numbness and sleep. At the cemetery gate she
took a deep breath. The old victoria separated her slowly from
her love. At the hill of Viridis the coachman slowed the horse to
a walk. This was the spot on the road where she always remembered having once met Bob, when he was a child, on his way
home from bathing, carrying his minute and dripping bathing-
shorts, and biting a black grape. She saw him again now. She
also saw that the blight had destroyed her neighbour's vines,

and rejoiced to think that Viridis had been spared. But she must see that Galbert gave them two more sprayings. Elisabeth Gornac had again become one of those dead who are carried down the stream of life.